Winter Goldfinch

* * *

"*Winter Goldfinch* is a Southern original. Jayne Wall's first dance with the pen is heartbreakingly lyrical. Her characters are so perfectly flawed and so delicately human, closing the book becomes harder with each turn of the page. This is everything you could hope for in a first novel."

—Eugene L. Tinklepaugh,
Washington Daily News

* * *

"Wall takes us on a journey of the seasons and the senses in this lyrical novel of families, their secrets, and the pain they share. *Winter Goldfinch* is filled with descriptive prose and realistic dialogue. Creating a world filled with finely-drawn characters, Wall captures such keen sense of place that the world becomes a character in its own right. A beautiful Southern novel of the best kind, Wall's artistic eye dexterously sets the scene and lets her characters imbue it with life."

—M. K. Graff, author
The Blue Virgin, and other novels.

* * *

"Engrossing and touching, Jayne Davis Wall's *Winter Goldfinch* is a literary treat rich with mesmerizing characters and Southern grace."

—S. I. Horvath, author
Caged Metal Feathers

Winter Goldfinch

***

"Jayne Davis Wall has written a wise and sensitive novel rooted in the South, with lyrical descriptions of nature, weather and place. The book moves back and forth in time, telling the story of an appealing, eccentric woman and her family. Exceptionally poignant are the relationships of the women in the family. The book explores what it is to be a mother, a daughter. Death, as well as life is an important theme here, but in no way is this novel of despair. The characters, intense in their feelings, sometimes ambivalent, often hurting, learn, change, and come together in the end with understanding, love and hope. In addition to creating memorable people, Ms. Wall creates memorable dogs. The dogs in this book are not like extras in a movie; they are an integral part of the story, individuals in their own right, part of what makes *Winter Goldfinch* such a very good read."

—Susan Cohen, author
The Liberated Couple and
other works under pseudonym
Elizabeth St. Claire, and
Pan Am 103 with husband
Daniel Cohen

***

"Set in Eastern North Carolina, *Winter Goldfinch* is a touching and evocative account of the stresses and eventual healing of a dysfunctional southern family."

—David Cox
The Pamlico News

***

"Jayne Davis Wall explores the complicated relationships between a mother and her grown children in this gentle novel, deftly evoking the pace and cadence of life in this Eastern North Carolina setting."

—Penny Round, feature writer
The Pamlico News

Winter Goldfinch

Jayne Davis Wall

Blue Moon Press
an imprint of Tortuga Pines Publishing
SouthCreek Media
Aurora, NC.

Blue Moon Press
an imprint of Tortuga Pines Publishing
SouthCreek Media
P. O. Box 97
Aurora, NC 27806

This book is a work of fiction. Names, characters, places and incidents either are the product of the author's imagination or are used fictitiously. Any resemblance to actual persons, living or dead, events, or locals is coincidental.

©Copyright 2007 by Jayne Davis Wall

ISBN 978-0-9793415-0-2
Library of Congress #2007922535

Cover Design: Beverly Gorman
Book Design: BMP

No part of this book may be reproduced in any form, or by any electronic or mechanical means, including information storage and retreaval systems, without written permission of the publisher, except by a reviewer who may quote brief passages in a review.

All rights reserved

visit our website at www.southcreekmedia.com

Printed in China

For my mother who might or might not have understood.

Winter Goldfinch

a novel

Jayne Davis Wall

1984. New Year's Day slid in on icy knees. It had snowed many of the cold, brittle December days, and the river was almost covered in thick ice crusted over in sea gull-trodden white, slushy by noon and already freezing up again by four o'clock. Only the channel ran free that winter.

Prologue

Winter Goldfinch

Mimi

In Mimosa Sims's yard, under two ancient oaks and many spindly pine trees, the ice and snow remained untouched by the afternoon's sun. Even the water lapped at the sandy edge of her long-dead lawn beneath ice undiminished by the now bright light. "Cold and dark," Mimosa said, though she could see the sun dancing on the chop farther out on the river.

She was snuggled in her favorite wing chair by the radiator under the big window in the den, thin legs thrown over one of its arms in an unlady-like slouch. The wrinkled white skin of her nearly naked body made her scarlet nails and toenails stand out like holly berries fallen on snow.

Fingering the pearl choker she always wore, Mimosa

sat waiting for her son and daughter and watching her birds. The thistle feeder was crowded with the goldfinches she loved the best. Feathers flying, the olive green winter birds vied for places on the six little perches. "Drab creatures," she announced to nobody, but she could see the Japanese quince was becoming pink against the snow. She smiled. Soon, she thought, the male birds will be golden. There will be forsythia and spirea and another spring.

The air in the room was laden with the heavy scent of the lavender and white stock arranged in the half dozen vases dotted around the den, and her house was very warm, the way she liked it. She was dressed only in a baggy pair of purple shorts and an old bathing suit top. Mimosa couldn't say why she had started to need this sensation of heat, but she felt surrounded, hemmed in, trapped this cold, cold winter, and she just did. "I like it, and that's just that," words she'd said many times in her life.

"There's a turkey and a good country ham, Beale." Mimosa was mumbling to herself—a habit that she had developed early in a lonely childhood.

Iona, the tall, middle-aged black woman who was there three days a week, had come in quietly and was slapping at nonexistent dust on the bookcases. She hardly knew whether Mimosa was speaking to her or to herself and answered according to her own whim since Mimosa, herself, seemed to make no distinction. "Sometime she ac' right crazy," she mumbled under her breath.

"I've made potato salad and tomato aspic, and, oh yes, pimiento cheese. Adeline loves that—or she used to. Sort of picnicky for this weather, but who knows how they eat now. Years since they were here, and Langley so close, too. Finally. Wouldn't come home without his twin, I reckon. A Mrs. Smith apple pie—best with vanilla ice cream. It's good but probably I should have, at least, let Brice make

Winter Goldfinch

that. Thought they'd be here by now. Well, they've missed lunch . . . one meal I don't have to worry about, anyhow." Mimosa sighed heavily and, collapsing again into her habitual slump, rested her silvery head against the back of the chair, mingling her curls with its blue and white chintz.

Then, as if she had suddenly remembered something crucial to her menu, Mimosa leaned forward, placing her bare feet squarely on the floor, and rested her chin in both her hands. "Let's see . . .," she said.

The agitation, though, came from other thoughts. She knew this, and she resumed speaking out loud. "Almost wish they'd leave me alone . . . so long since they both were here . . . Addie in Spain with that sorry husband of hers and with a sick baby . . . see what all that nonsense came to . . . poor thing . . . never even saw it . . . my only grandbaby . . . and Langley off in Mexico, the Lord knows where . . . everybody just gone . . . me without anybody."

"That was before I worked here, Miz Mimosa."

Iona finished the dusting and began to bundle the vacuum cleaner cord.

Mimosa had caught her attention with this new information.

"Well, I swanee, it was awful", Mimosa continued. "Everybody died at once. Lillian had been dead so long by then that I'd almost gotten right . . . then bang . . . the children's daddy, even Addie's husband and her sweet little baby . . . all in those horrible years. Adeline buried both of hers over there in Spain and didn't come back till after her daddy's funeral, and, even then, I had to go up to New York to see her after Charlie died, when she finally did get herself back in the country."

"Uh, huh, that is bad, but now you got that nice Mr. Brice. He sure take good care of you. I bet he half your age . . . now ain't you something," Iona spoke in the easy familiarity they both had become accustomed to, the one not noticing and the other used to not being noticed.

"Yes. Brice is just about too good to be true, cooking when he's here and carrying me around whenever he can, and, tell you the truth, I almost wish they'd just go back and leave me alone. I miss them so much, but all this cooking has just about worried me to death. I'm plumb worn out, but I wanted to do all of it for them. I did, too, all of it. Brice didn't do any," and Mimosa continued to talk to the empty room while Iona took the flowers, vase by vase, to the kitchen to freshen the water.

"Cut the ends off the stems and add another aspirin." Mimosa broke off her mumblings and raised her voice.

"Yes'm," Iona answered and added to herself. "She bout to worry me to death, too. I been doing that same thing all this winter."

*

Winter Goldfinch

1955 Lillian

Lillian lay back on the blue and white ticking of the pillows propped against the wall. The bed, itself, was unmade and rumpled and soiled. A microcosm of the squalid room.

The chipped porcelain sink was crowded with unwashed dishes sitting in gray, greasy water.

The trashcan, overflowing with Chinese take-out cartons, was buzzing with flies stirring the fetid air as they came and went through a broken pane of the single, grimy window.

The bed sheets tumbled to the floor on one side leaving the other side of the stained mattress uncovered, the stuffing hardly contained where missing buttons had left jagged holes.

Lillian felt no repugnance for the bed, the filthy, disordered room or her trapped dark life. She felt herself lifting from the bed and floating, then melting, warm and liquid, her body spreading itself, everywhere over the universe.

I was brave, she thought. She had used the last he had and she knew she would pay, but her need had overcome her fear, and, now, how delicious, how quiet, how warm.

Her limbs loosened and fell away from her body and her mind went far away.

She smells honeysuckle and pine resin and feels sun warm on her face . . . soft tar under her feet.

There is Mae Pearl in her little round eyeglasses and the white socks falling down around her thin, brown ankles.

She pushes the twins in their stroller down the hill to the park. Lillian is ten. She hops with one dirty little foot and then the other on the hot asphalt.

"Pal, come off the street. Stay on the grass." She calls to her small dog.

"Whyn't you wore yo shoes?" She hears Mae fussing in her head and herself answer.

"The twins are barefooted."

"Well, they ain't gonna walk, is dey?"

Lillian sees herself there among the little party meandering lazily up into the pinewoods following the sandy path that begins at the edge of the park. "Les go up in the cool. Dem big boys is all over the swings right now. We ken do that on the way home.

"Swing low, sweet chariot, a comin' for to carry me home. Swi-ing low, sweet chariot . . . ."

"La, la, la." Lillian, humming along, hears herself and Mae Pearl's rich, sweet voice blend with the sound of catbirds whispering in the vines which climb the trees along

Winter Goldfinch

the path, and, then as suddenly as if it were happening again, she feels her heart stop at the strange animal noise in the woods.

Pal, the little brown and white terrier, is standing his ground protecting them all from whatever crackles and growls in the woods.

She sees again Mae Pearl screaming and crying. "Oh Lord Jesus!" Mae turning and running, her rubbery arms and legs flying everywhere, her socks flopping up and down as if they would become wings to fly her out of danger. She pushes and drags the stroller, the twins bouncing this way and that, in great danger of ending on the ground, and screaming bloody murder. "Lillian, run, run! Lordy Jesus! He gonna eat you up! Run!"

Lillian remembers fierce little Pal would not run. She had been brave that day, too. The big boys had had their fun with them, but she had been as brave as Pal, dragging him as she ran with her wobbly, jelly knees.

She pulls and half carries her little dog to the safety of the park and follows, running, leaving the big boys laughing their guts out still in the woods. Mae Pearl is already way up the hill and almost home when Lillian, safe, stops to wipe her nose and streaming eyes on the hem of her dress and scowls at the boys before she turns to trot home quickly after her nurse.

In the warm dark, Lillian felt herself, safe again and peaceful, slip over an edge into a velvet comfort.

She couldn't hear the voice roaring at her from the doorway. "You stinking bitch," it bellowed. She couldn't feel the rough hands grabbing her arms and dragging the dead weight of her flopping body out of bed and, when her head banged again and again against the cracked plaster of the sordid little room, the universe simply folded itself into ebony black and disappeared.

*

Jayne Davis Wall

1964 Langley

Once the rain started, the water became still. He had seen it slanting across the river even before the low whisper song of the catbird had stopped and he heard the first deafening crack of thunder. In that silence before the rain turned the world into sound, he was suddenly engulfed in a sweet white scent so palpable he felt he could touch it, hold it in his hand and bury his face in it. "Honeysuckle," he whispered.

*

Winter Goldfinch

1964 Addie

Her feet can just touch the tepid brown water, quiet and warm again after the rain. The sun shines hot on her back. The wind lifts her hair and dries the sweat on her neck.

There are fish, she knows. She smells the bream spawning near shore.

She loves this place under the pine tree.

She looks at the little silver ring, twists it off her finger and drops it into a crack in the retaining wall.

There is a satisfying plonk as it hits the water trapped within the broken bricks.

"A sacrifice."

She closes her eyes, lifting her face to the warm sun and crosses the fingers of both her hands, smiling into the heat. "Now," she sighs.

*

Jayne Davis Wall

**Part I
Beginning**

Jayne Davis Wall

Winter Goldfinch

Thanksgiving 1983

Addie felt the platter slip out of her soapy hands. She juggled to save it, but, even as she did, she knew it was lost. The little platter, "just big enough for a small turkey . . . enough for two people," her mother-in-law had said as Addie carefully folded the bright Christmas paper on her lap . . . only she and John knowing she was already pregnant.

A lifetime ago.

She stood for a moment looking down at the broken pieces, the little goldfinch in flight, the violets that had twined around the rim, which were now in fragments on the speckled linoleum, and then, she knelt in her tiny kitchen and piled the small broken pieces on top of the largest one, the heart of the plate. The little fluttering goldfinch was almost whole but for the long crack that ran diagonally across its breast.

Carefully she walked on her knees over to the trashcan under the sink and tipped in the pieces.

She sat back on her heels, ran her hand over the floor, and, finding no slivers there, she stood and wiped her hands on her jeans.

"So, that's an end to it, then," she said aloud.

*

Winter Goldfinch

**Part Two
Home Again**

ns Wall

Winter Goldfinch

Addie 1984

Today was Monday, two days into the New Year.

At mid-morning a shaggy black dog, all four feet splayed in different directions on the icy street, collided with a skidding car on Center Avenue and was thrown through the air at the feet of three little boys standing, frozen in horror, on the sidewalk.

When he rose from his furry heap and ran limping and yelping off across the front yards and around the corner, the children ran after, calling to him and squealing with surprise and thankful glee.

Adeline Sims stood and watched, first with horror, herself, and then with a great sigh of relief. She was standing across the street by a gas pump at the Exxon station on the corner of Center and Fourth Street, shaking in the brittle air under the same large water oak that had left the street frozen and was now shielding her from even the wan winter sun. Her legs were still weak from the scene she had witnessed, and she shivered.

A mixed flock of starlings and grackles started up from where someone had scattered seed on the sidewalk and perched above her head in the great old tree beside the street. Their shiny iridescence flickered through the branches as one or the other happened into a random ray of sun. They were ruffled with the cold and complaining in a group clatter from their freezing perch in the tree.

"Yeah, me too, but, please, no more omens!"

The last time she had been home, Lillian had been already dead for ten years, Addie thought, and she shivered again. Her glamorous older sister, mysterious and beautiful, dead, her throat opened with a straight razor, and left to bleed out in a bathtub. Addie and Langley, thirteen years old, and absorbed in their nascent teenage fog, had been told nothing of this. Lillian was dead, they knew. The few questions they asked were met with resolute silence. Little scraps had been gathered by listening to the grown-ups talking quietly in their living room, while the twins were thought to be sleeping in their next-door bedrooms. And, so, like half-remembered snatches of a dream, they had learned only scattered bits of their sister's story.

On that last trip home, Daddy, she thought, had been alive too, and Mimi had been trying not to drink then, sucking on diet ginger ale in the evenings and swinging back and forth in the glider on the screened porch.

Back then Addie had been engaged to John. Boy, did that ever throw Mimi for a loop and put her right back on the jug. Oh, well. Don't think about all that. Just don't. Sometime the dog survives.

Winter Goldfinch

"Maybe Mimi will still be sober," she said out loud and stuck both numbed hands into her pockets as she fumbled for her gloves. Pulling them on, she turned back to her car where her twin brother, Langley, was waiting in the passenger seat, unaware of the drama in the street. He was smoking and listening to the radio, the smoke and the beat spilling out of the cracked window. She could see him nodding and slapping his knee in time to something she couldn't quite hear. Typical, she thought, off in his own world.

"Come on, let's go." Rolling his window all the way down, Langley laughed and dropped his cigarette out for her to step on.

"Glad I'm here to serve you, Langley," she said. "Thank the Lord you didn't blow us up with that butt. You're really a hazard."

She slid under the steering wheel and started the car with her dog pawing her from the backseat and licking her neck. "Stop it, Fitz. It won't be long now."

Addie was cold and irritable, but she gently pushed the little terrier back into the seat and flipped the heater on full blast, even though it would take a few minutes to warm up, and carefully pulled into the icy street.

"Give it a second," Langley said, turning the heater off again, "you're always pushing things too fast."

She knew he was right.

What a way to start a new year, she thought. "My God," she muttered under her breath.

"You also think too much," her brother said, answering her sigh. "Look at me. Happy as a lark to be back."

"You are not. Who do you think you're kidding?" She paused, frowning at her brother. "Really, though, we've got to talk before we get there."

"Yeah. Anyhow, let's stop at that Sizzler up a ways and get a cup of coffee. I'm cold to the bone."

Adeline was chilled, too, and wanted to walk her dog again before she got to her mother's. Perish the thought he'd tinkle in Mimi's house.

In the restaurant parking lot, their icy breath white around their heads, Addie and Langley watched Fitz make a quick tour of the shrubbery bordering the asphalt, locked him back in the car and hurried out of the cold.

They settled into the warmth of a soft upholstered booth where they could watch the car and ordered coffee. Altered by the cold or his own thoughts, Langley had lost hold of his earlier gaiety and answered "yep" and "nope" to any attempt at conversation. Addie pulled a tangerine out of her coat pocket and began to peel it into the ashtray on the table.

"Want some?"

"Nope."

"Okay, I'll leave you alone in a minute, but I'm serious." The look she gave him was solemn and unwavering. "We have to talk now so we won't have to do it in front of Mimi. I've already looked into the Methodist Home in Durham just in case, and Fluffy Trueblood down at the bank will take care of everything with Mimi's stock if we do have to put her there.

"Langley, are you listening?" She could tell his mind was wandering. Looking down at his hands, he was raising, then lowering, the same fingers of each hand starting with his pinkies and working toward his thumbs.

"I give up. Damn it! If you really don't care . . . .." Addie trailed off and shifted in the booth for the first time since they had sat down. She leaned forward and put both her hands on her brother's larger freckled ones to stop the action of his fingers and draw his attention.

"Look, I've told you a million times," he said. "I don't care. I won't be any help because I'll be back in Raleigh." He withdrew his hands, but his eyes stayed on hers. "I prom-

Winter Goldfinch

ise I'll visit and all, but you make the decisions. I'll go along with whatever you think is best. Just don't jump the gun. You only have Coralee's nosy word for any of this. Mimi may be fine."

    Addie slipped out of her coat and settled back, sighing. He was right, of course. All right, but, just in case . . .. She knew what had to be done, and she was content—enough. Yes. She knew the things she'd have to do. The house. The furniture. Store the good pieces. Close up everything. Something though . . . what about the drinking . . . what if . . .. Just then, a Bradford pear tree in the parking lot caught her eye and held her thought. It was flashing with handsome winter birds. Cedar waxwings. They were greedy, feeding on the little pear-berries still clinging to the frozen bare branches, and, in their haste, were littering the already soiled snow around the base of the tree with a scattering of their crumbs.

    They reminded her, immediately, of the cardinals that nested in the spring under the den window at home. Mimi watching from her chair. Mother's cardinals. Fluttering in the street in a frantic mating dance one minute. Smashed flat the next. Both of them. Poor Mimi. She never sat on the street side of the house after that. She had taken the bedroom on the water to sit in and she and Daddy had made the den their bedroom, closing the heavy drapes against the day as well as the night.

    Langley signaled the waitress for refills and Addie looked back at her brother, left alone to sip his coffee and mope. Coffee white with cream and so sweet that she could almost smell the sugar. He was a large man, tall and only slightly muscular. He takes up so much space, she thought. Slouching there in the padded booth he radiated a sort of loose-jointed male assertiveness that was attractive.

    Women sometimes told him he was handsome, she knew, and, with his light hair curling behind his neat close ears and his shy hazel eyes, he was handsome, but something furtive and retreating was there in his eyes as well, and women turned away from him without even guessing that he was gay. Some sort of self-preservation, she thought. Addie had known for a long time, though Langley had never ever talked seriously to her about it, and she thought, maybe, Mimi did, too, though the subject would certainly be taboo with her. He's rangy like daddy was and I'm little like Mother, she mused. Constantly dieting. "See me using sugar." Adeline's mind wandered, dipping here and there. Thinking of her mother and what had been set in motion by her Aunt Coralee's tattletale letter.

"Things like that," she had said, "just don't look nice. She's about worried us to death." Coralee was always worried about somebody's business and Mimi had worried Addie to death her whole life. The two of them never seemed to get along. Addie was Daddy's little girl, always. She didn't want to even try to please Mimi anymore, or to rehash her marriage for that matter, and Addie had wanted to just tune out the whole problem. She certainly didn't want to come home, but who else would take care of her mother? Langley sure wouldn't, even though he lived so near to Windley. He steered clear of Mimi, too.

Feeling sorry for herself, Addie felt tears prick and blew her nose with a crumpled tissue. All this planning. Please let it be for nothing, she prayed silently, determined to rid her mind of all this she'd thought about since she first opened her aunt's letter. She closed her eyes and began to listen to snatches of conversation she could barely hear from the booth in front of theirs. This was a game she often played. Willing herself to be entertained, she strained to hear and fell immediately out of her world into another.

One voice was full and fruity with a trace of whiskey and cigarettes.

" . . . wanted his ashes scattered to the four winds off

Winter Goldfinch

the top of Pike's Peak."

    One voice was younger and touched with innocence. "Ain't that in Colorado?"

    ". . . somewhere out there . . . didn't inherit nothing because . . .."

    "I knew somebody . . .."

    ". . . her uterus had shriveled up to the size of a . . .."

    ". . . suffered for years...way to die . . .."

    Langley shifted in the booth and the sudden movement along with the clinking of his spoon as he stirred yet more sugar into his coffee brought Adeline back. She glanced through the window at the car and saw Fitz scrabbling at the glass on the driver's side, barking non-stop at a man walking a fat collie across the parking lot. The man, who was reasonably tall, she thought, was laughing his head off at Fitz as he put his dog into an old green station wagon.

    He entered the warm restaurant pushing icy air toward her as he moved but, before she had time to check out this fellow who seemed to like dogs as well as she, the conversation emanating from the next booth caught her attention once again.

    ". . . say she crazy as a bedbug . . .."

    ". . . walk all over town scattering birdseed and bread and in her bathrobe, too . . . this . . . weather . . .."

    ". . . uh-huh, I know . . .."

    ". . . birds all round her head . . .."

    ". . . yeah, I seen her once at the Piggly Wiggly . . .."

    "Let's go." This was Langley and Addie jumped a little, startled, as he unfolded himself and stood up to leave. "I'll pay. You tip," he ordered.

    Addie, jerked back into her own world, cast an interested look at the dog lover now seated at the counter and gave only a quick glance at the two women in the forward booth. She found her keys, dropped a dollar on the table, and, buttoning her coat, joined her brother at the door.

By the time they were on the street again, it was after one o'clock.

They drove, still quiet, watching the neighborhoods melting one into the other. Houses they had known all their childhood years. Not much had changed. The large houses still there and a few banks and law offices. Not many people on the street, Addie thought, way too cold.

Going carefully under the oaks, where the street was still icy, until the big trees began to dwindle and give way to younger, leafless trees and smaller houses. Here everything seemed to change, and a shimmery light pulsed through the thin trees as they moved along. Faster now.

The sun was beginning to win over and melting ice and snow had begun to pour from eaves and run in gutters. Every naked twig was sparkling now with rivulets of water dripping quickly in the thin sunshine. It was as if the whole town was dissolving and running off somewhere.

"We had fun here, didn't we?" She wasn't really asking and Langley didn't answer. His thoughts were elsewhere she knew, but he surprised her.

"Turn here," he said.

"Why?"

"I want to get out at the corner and walk the rest of the way."

She turned off Center Avenue onto Jackson and stopped the car.

"It's obvious we didn't come from the same egg," she said, "but, okay, hop out. Get your parka or you'll freeze to death." He got out without comment or his coat and slammed the passenger door too hard. Fitz jumped into the front seat and, paws on the dash, watched Langley move away, his arms swinging and his shining head bent into his hunched shoulders.

What a dope, she thought, and quickly drove past

Winter Goldfinch

him.

"Good luck!" She threw the words against the closed window and saw his plaid shirt slip across the rear view mirror and disappear as she turned right on Trent Lane toward the river.

*

Jayne Davis Wall

Home Sweet Home

Addie pulled into her mother's driveway behind a battered red Buick, gravel crunching under the brittle snow, which appeared disturbed by cars coming and going that day. Addie's heart thumped in her chest. "Damn it. I need Langley. I should have just gone to a motel and let him get here first . . . oh, crap, come on, Fitz, we'll just have to go in."

She pulled on the emergency brake and stuck the key in her coat pocket. Snapping the lead onto the dog's collar, she put him under her arm so his feet would stay dry and, slipping a little on the icy walk, started toward the house. She didn't knock. She knew Mimosa would be on the riverside of the house.

Winter Goldfinch

Pushing hard against the heavy oak door, "Mimi," she called. "My god, it's hot in here. What in the world?"

She put Fitz down on the bare floor, his nails making a clacking sound as he sought his footing.

"Here you are, Adeline." Mimi rushed into the living room, her naked feet slipping silently along the bare floor. "Oh, I've missed you." Mimosa allowed herself to be embraced. "Come in and take off your coat. It's plenty warm in here. I didn't know you were bringing a dog. Where's Langley? Why don't you put the dog out on the porch?" Mimosa's words tumbled over each other, but, all the while, she was watching Fitz as he sniffed around the legs of the few chairs in the living room.

"Mimi, where's the furniture? My gosh, the place is practically empty. What happened?"

"Well, now, I just didn't need all that old stuff and this man came by and offered me a pretty good price for everything I didn't want, so I sold it. I've got tons of furniture in my bedroom and the den and then I furnished Brice's room with all new stuff from Heilig and Meyers when they were having one of their going-out-of-business sales. That's your old room, but I kept some other beds, Langley's twins and one in both guestrooms."

Addie was feeling faint. "My old room? And who's Brice?"

"Oh," Mimosa said, "oh, you haven't met him yet. Let's get the little dog on the porch. Oh, here's Iona. Iona, come meet my precious daughter, Adeline. Adeline, this is Iona. She keeps house for me." Mimi relaxed visibly when the black woman appeared and Addie felt herself do the same.

"Hey, Iona," Adeline said. "I think I must be blocking your car."

"It's okay for now," Iona said. "I still have to vacuum the bedrooms. It's nice to meet you." She smiled widely.

"It's nice to meet you, too, Iona. Is it always this hot in here?" Addie met her smile in kind and offered her hand.

"Yes ma'am. Your mama need to move down to Florida so she can keeps warm in the wintertime. She play like she at the beach when it snow."

"God, Mother, this is horrible. How do you stand it? Oh, I see." Suddenly, taking stock of Mimi's clothing, Addie stood back with her still-gloved hands over her mouth and her eyebrows raised in alarm. "It's so hot in here that I hadn't even noticed your crazy clothes." She dropped her hands into her pockets. Remain calm, she advised herself.

"Well, I like it and my clothes are just right for inside. It makes me feel cozy to be nice and warm. Take off some of those heavy things of yours, and you'll be more comfortable. Now let's get this dog on the porch."

"Mimi, Fitz is an inside dog. He can't stay on the porch in this weather. You knew I had a dog. He's trained. He's not going to hurt a thing, but, as hot as it is, we'll probably both be sick. Can't you turn the heat down a little?"

Ignoring her daughter's question but not making a move to oust Fitz, Mimosa asked again, "I thought Langley was coming with you. Where is he?"

"Mimi, I'm not Langley's keeper, though God knows he needs one. I can probably guess where he is, but so can you." Addie shed her coat, her scarf, her gloves, pulled her sweater over her head, and, after looking around the room for a place to put them, dropped them on the floor.

"Oh, shoot, I have to move the car. This is totally nuts, Mimi." She began to bundle up again.

"Well, I like it." Mimi turned away. "It makes me feel good, and I don't go out much anymore in the cold weather."

Fitz beat Addie to the door. "Maybe he would enjoy being out on the porch," Mimi said, but Addie ignored her.

"An insane asylum," she said to herself as she started the car and backed down the drive to give Iona room to

Winter Goldfinch

turn her car around when she was ready to leave.

Looking in the rear view mirror, she saw Langley trudging dejectedly toward her. She jumped out of the car with Fitz on her hip.

"You're looking a little frozen there, bro, but don't worry. You'll soon thaw out. It's 110 degrees inside. You'll be as cozy as Mimi in no time at all."

"What are you talking about?" Langley scowled at her.

"Come inside and see," Addie answered struggling to open the heavy paneled front door with Fitz wriggling in one arm.

"Langley!" Mimosa stood smiling in the now open door. "I'm so glad you're home. Come in. Come in. Where in the world have you been?'

"Hi, Mimi." He hugged her, her head coming to his armpit. "How are you, shorty? I just needed some air. My God! Is the house on fire? Have I entered the gates of hell or what?" Both Addie and Langley were now struggling out of their warm clothing and dropping their assorted articles on the floor. Fitz, panting juicily, climbed on top of the pile and collapsed with a sigh. "My God, Mimi, where's all the furniture? And what's with the get-up?" Langley looked around, puzzled.

Mimosa tried to smile at him, but her lips trembled. "I like a good warm house, Langley, and we have plenty of furniture. Maybe Iona could bring in your bags before she leaves so you won't have to bundle up again. I don't know why you didn't bring them inside in the first place," but Langley had already started out the door.

"I'll go. I need some more air," he said and fanned his face, sticking out his tongue in a fake pant.

*

Jayne Davis Wall

Addie

Sweating and dragging her wheeled case down the long hall leading from the foyer past, first, her old bedroom, then Langley's bedroom, Adeline could hear Iona vacuuming in Mimi's room next to the guestroom where she was to sleep. She walked in with Fitz trailing behind and threw her brown canvas suitcase onto the bed. She unzipped the cover and rummaged inside looking for something cooler to wear.

This room, at least, was familiar. The guest room. Winter sun through the slatted blinds cast barred light across the snowy spread on the high mahogany bed and on the blue satin comforter folded at its foot. Blue and pink hooked rugs were scattered as they had been in her childhood. Polished floor, gray woodwork, wallpaper with its twining pink bows and small blue flowers . . . a girl's room really . . . "but not my room," she mused. "Who is this Brice, for God's sake?" she said aloud. Her dark hair plastered to her forehead and sweat trickling down her back and between her shoulder blades, she slammed herself, bouncing, onto the bed, her feet dangling, and pushed her boots, one at a time, off onto the floor.

"Poor Fitzgerald." She looked down at her dog who had given up trying to climb up onto the bed and had stretched his short legs out on the bare floor under the bed out of the reach of the afternoon sun. "Maybe you would be better off on the porch. No, this is crazy. There must be a thermostat somewhere." She stomped in her sock feet out into the hall where Iona was finishing her vacuuming. "Oh, hey, Iona. Where is the thermostat? I can't stand this."

Stooping, Iona turned off the vacuum and started to coil the cord. "It right there next to the bathroom door, but she don't like nobody to touch it. Mr. Brice bought a fan for his room and you prob'ly got one in yo' closet, too."

Adeline peered at the thermostat in the dim light of the hall. "Good Lord, it's set at 86 degrees! Maybe, if I just turn it down gradually, she won't notice."

"She gonna notice, Miss Adeline, but she might not fuss too much, it being you and Mr. Langley. She glad to see you after such a long time." Iona leaned against the handle of the Hoover, still holding the coiled cord. Her seamed face glistened with damp and the whites of her dark eyes seemed to pop with their brightness.

"I'm just turning it down two degrees. If I live, I'll turn it down two more tomorrow, and, maybe, we can get some clothes on her."

"Yes'm, she right near stark neckid," Iona agreed with her wide smile.

Jayne Davis Wall

Addie stuck her hands in her pockets and rested one shoulder against the wall. Her dog, dragging his lead, joined them and plopped down with his head on Addie's foot. "Iona, how long has this been going on and who the heck is this Brice in my bedroom?"

Iona dropped the cord into place on the machine and leaned against the wall, mirroring Adeline. She was ready to get down to business. "Well, Mr. Brice, he the new sheriff in Windley County, and your mama had a little bit of trouble one day with her car in a ditch or somethin' and, I think, trespassin' on some farmer's property when she was pickin' Queen Anne's lace like she do in the summertime, and they just like hit it off . . . your mama having all this big house and him staying down to that Golden Weed Motel, 'bout to fall down now an' all . . . him being so new in town."

Iona's words were falling too fast on Addie, and her mind was reeling. "The sheriff . . . and, just like that . . . my room . . . but . . . how long has he been here?"

Iona grinned. "Well, first, Miss Jewell took yo' mama to the country club fo' some party, weddin', I think, and Mr. Brice was there, and they was dancing . . . yo' know how good yo' mama love to dance, I bet." Addie nodded with her mouth open not knowing what to ask next. "Well, Mr. Brice, it turn out, is a fine dancing gentlemens his own self, and, after they dance . . . that was that . . . and, tell you the truth, Miss Adeline, he mighty sweet on yo' mama, and he treat her right good, too." Iona smiled like the sun at Addie who shut her eyes and shook her head. "Two years he been here, now," she said. "Don't you worry, Miss Adeline, he do treat her good." Looking over to check the cord again, Iona abruptly tilted the cleaner on its wheels and turned to go. "Well, reckon I better stop my gossip and get on home 'fore everything start freezin' up again . . . see y'all Wednesday . . .," she chirped and pushed her

Winter Goldfinch

ancient machine down the hall leaving Addie still leaning in the darkening light.

"Trespassing, well," she said, "Mimi always did pick ditch bank flowers wherever she found them . . . follow them right along like Hansel and Gretel following breadcrumbs . . . serve her right if this Brice had put her in jail."

Addie left the hall with Fitz panting along behind. She found a pair of nylon running shorts and a cotton tee shirt, which she slipped into.

Sitting on the bed, one foot across her other knee, she pulled a sock off, let it drop to the floor and pressed her small hands against her knees as both feet again dangled. Her shoulders hunched. Her head sank and she became quiet and still. There was a clock ticking loudly somewhere down the hall, a radio playing off in the other part of the house, her own heart beating. Fitz sighed. Outside the insistent drip, drip, drip of an icicle, which had formed above the window, was like pinpricks to her nerves. "What am I doing," she said softly. "Why are we here?" Fitz pricked up his ears, listening. "Last time she was drunk as a skunk, breathing Chablis all in my face and trying to fix my hair with those horrid combs she used to wear and insisting I try on her crummy clothes. And, God, those combs had to be left over from the forties. Awful. 'Take off those dungarees and try this on, honey.' Hadn't been out of the house to shop for ten years. Ugh. That morning I had been so happy, sitting by the river...and then, bam! Telling her I was marrying John just made her crazy. I'll give her this, though, she did get herself under control before the week was over. She kept trying to 'talk sense' into me all summer, but she stayed sober until after I left to go to John in Spain. Oh, well . . . .."

Addie shook herself, reached down, unhooked her dog's lead, and, tossing it onto the bed, went in search of Langley.

*

Jayne Davis Wall

Langley 1952

It is raining. Langley peers through the lavender clusters of crepe myrtle arching over the stone bench where he waits for the July rain to stop. The big splashy drops of the summer shower pelt down everywhere, plopping like so many bullfrogs on the surface of the deep ditch behind him, which is already beginning to swell with the run-off, and onto the leaves and pine needles on the ground all around and through the broad leaves of the jack oaks above him. But Langley is practically dry. A sweet-smelling vine his mother called virgin's bower had grown up through the branches of the crepe myrtle and woven them together until they were almost impenetrable. Honeysuckle, he thinks, is there too, a summer fragrance he knows well,

Winter Goldfinch

and he breathes deep into the rainy intenseness of it. Birds nest there and he hears many little scratchings and rustling sounds, though he can't see the birds. He has sheltered on this bench many times this summer, and when winter comes, he will see their nests in the bare trees.

He will look for them then, though he rarely takes nests anymore.

Last year, when he was seven, he found a bluebird's nest in the hollow of a tree near the road in front of his house. He broke some of the rotted wood away so he could peep into the nest and so disturbed the parent birds that they deserted their babies.

Langley found them dead and wet with dew early the next morning.

He dreamed about them afterwards at night for a long time, called out to them in his sleep, and scared Mimi when he walked in his sleep out to the screened porch and tried to go off into the night.

Now he is a big boy, though, and he hardly thinks about them anymore.

He is eight this year and allowed to roam all around, wherever he wants to go. Mostly, he wants to be on the end of his family's pier or in the water where it isn't over his head. He is, his mother says, "brown as a berry," and his hair, blond, even in winter, is bleached almost completely white in the summer sun.

He is barefoot all this summer and one of his toes is still bloody from this morning's collision with a tree root. Both knees are scabbed from a recent backwards slide down the side of the ditch bank.

He wears only a faded blue bathing suit, its tie-string loose and dangling between his legs now. He had worn the suit ever since school let out, slept in it, even. Why should he wear anything else? He is usually on the pier fishing or trying to catch crabs with a string and a soup bone, pulling them along slow and slow, hand over hand until he can quickly scoop one into the long-handled net and dump it into his bucket. The hard thing is getting those strong claws to let go of the net. Langley is good at this part but often a big crab drops off on the pier mad as fire and ready to fight. They always ended up dropping off into the river, and, anyway, Mimi makes him dump them all at the end of the day. Not the fish. She fries them for supper, the pretty robins and perch and the golden croakers begging, it seems to Langley, in their strange voices for release. Mimi always calls Mr. Thomas at Thomas's Seafood Safari for crabmeat. Dressing crabs is too much work and hard on Mimi's hands.

Sometimes Langley likes to play in the woods up the hill from where he is now in the park. There the white sand is soft and cool under his feet where the path is shaded by the tall pine trees on either side. Back in the woods are clearings where he and his best friend, Buddy, or maybe Cordon, pretend to camp, making pine straw beds and, sometimes, little structures for shelter where the trees are close enough together and they can find long branches.

Sometimes Addie comes with him, but not as much now that they are allowed to roam all over. She'd rather play with all girls.

Today he is meeting his second best friend, Cordon Wheeler. Early this morning, Cordon, called him on the telephone and said, "I'll meet you at the bench at 1:30, okay?"

Langley left early, walking. His bicycle has flat tires, as usual, and now Cordon is probably caught at home not wanting to ride his new bike in the rain. Langley doesn't care. He likes sitting here, listening to the rain. He leans back against the hard bench, pulls his feet up off the wet leaves and begins to whistle a tune his daddy taught him and Addie when they were so little that they sang in babytalk . . .. "And tars fwell on Amabama wast nwight" . . .

Winter Goldfinch

they'd sing in the middle of the living room with lamp light shining on their heads, and Mimi and Daddy would laugh and hug them both and ask them to sing again.

*

Jayne Davis Wall

Mimi and Fitz

Langley sat in his old room. Leaning back in a chair belonging to the desk that had once been his daddy's, then his own when Grandmother died, he propped his feet on one of his boyhood twin beds, the one where he'd always slept. He looked past it through the windows that faced out on the snow-covered lawn, past the trees and to the bright river, still lit by the falling sun.

He was thinking about Mrs. Slater. She had welcomed him with open arms as usual. Seeing her was like returning to the womb, he thought.

He had never wanted to come back here. He didn't want his old friends. He didn't want the old scenery, the memories, the thoughts that haunted his dreams, and, for

Winter Goldfinch

reasons he couldn't articulate, even to himself, he especially didn't want Mimi. He did want Mrs. Slater, though, now that he was here. He wanted to sit on her couch, with his feet on her old coffee table, drink beer and smoke cigarettes with her and maybe play cards like the gang of them used to.

Even more he wanted to be a little boy again playing in her backyard with her little boy, Buddy . . . before Langley understood the true gravity of what had happened and before the haunting began to darken his waking thoughts, as well as his dreams. Before Mrs. Slater understood how the terrible thing that happened had crippled him and she had become, first, a confessor of sorts and then, once, but only once, his lover . . . her compassion and her own loneliness driving her to try to fix him. I had to see her first, he thought. Her warmth. Even now their equal need. And the poor little sex, he remembered, from so long ago, had been essentially innocent, just a coming together in a forlorn bid for comfort, however sad and brief.

"You look lost in thought," Addie said, entering after only a quiet rap on the open door. "Same old room, cowboys and indians. Guess she couldn't stand to let go of her baby boy. You should re-decorate. Wouldn't that be fun, now? Let's see . . . some silk and satin . . . some naked boy statues . . . a dressing table with movie star lights and an organdy skirt . . . ."

"Shut-up, Addie." Langley smiled, ready to be tugged out of his reverie. "She must know I'm gay. It probably wouldn't shock her if I did go pink. She knows. She just won't talk about it; besides, she's the one off her nut."

Langley had found a fan in his closet and set it tilted down slightly, on the dresser between the beds. The breeze oscillating around the room ruffled his hair, then the curtains, red and dotted with spurs and lassos. The little breeze passed to the chenille bedspread on one bed and then the other until it reached Addie seated at the foot of the second bed, and a few drying strands of her hair lifted and fell as the breeze fanned back the other way.

"That feels good," Addie said, "Mimi may have something. It does feel like summer. Wonder if I have a fan in my closet."

Fitz, looking for the coolest spot, settled on the bare floor by the desk.

Outside the sun was westering and the liquid sounds of only an hour earlier were beginning to quiet as the ice re-formed and the light disappeared. Langley reached behind him and switched on his desk lamp, its rearing horse and rider springing out of shadow.

Looking toward the desk, Addie said, "You know, I loved horses . . . more than you did and for longer, but Mimi wouldn't let Daddy get me a pony. Scared I'd get hurt. Remember when we used to ride those brooms all over the place?"

"I remember a lot of stuff," Langley answered, yawning and stretching his arms toward the ceiling.

"You look so much like Daddy," Addie said, watching him. "Were you at Mrs. Slater's?" She asked without expecting an answer.

But Langley looked up at her and simply shook his head. "Yes", he said. "You and Mimi, and probably the whole town, disapproved of her, I know, but she was always just a nice lonely woman who made her house comfortable for us boys." He looked a challenge at his sister, but, before Addie could answer, their mother appeared in the doorway.

"Well, here you are. I'm glad to see you're dressed a little cooler." Mimi arrived silently from the hall on her bare feet. She had changed into red Bermuda shorts and a white sleeveless shirt. Dressing for dinner, Langley thought sarcastically.

Winter Goldfinch

"Fitz, no," Addie was up grabbing, at his collar. He was licking Mimi's toes and dancing around her thin legs, tongue hanging out in a smile of pure joy. "I'm afraid he's fallen for you, Mimi," Addie smirked.

"Dogs always like me," Mimi said," I just don't like to have them inside . . . but, well . . . he is a nice little dog. He just took me by surprise. We haven't had a dog in so long. Remember Danny, your Aunt Grace's dog?"

"They're the same, Mimi, Scottish terriers."

"Uncle Julie used to put that dog on one knee and you on the other and sing "Danny Boy", or was it "Sonny Boy", to you both. A cute, silly man, when he was sober, and awful to Grace when he wasn't. Oh dear, Grace was better off without him." No one spoke for a minute while family and the past intruded into the warm, dim room and huddled around, bringing them at once within touching distance of one another.

Fitz, untroubled by ghosts, licked Mimi's toes again, breaking the little spell, and Mimi said, "Oh, all right, Fitz, let's all go and meet Brice."

*

Jayne Davis Wall

Addie, Langley, and Brice Darden

Addie and Langley followed Mimi down the long hall leading to the living room, across another hall, the house meandering as old added-on-to houses do, and into the den which was even more sweltering than the other wing of the house had been.

"Children, I want you to meet Brice, Brice Darden. Brice, my children, Adeline and Langley," Mimi said, leaning away from the three of them. She anchored herself against a desk standing by the door of the kitchen and busied herself with re-arranging the flower vase on its upper level before she moved behind them and sat on the edge of her chair. She hunched forward with her fingers tightly entwined, corralling her knees.

Winter Goldfinch

"Hello, Brice," Addie said, trying to hide the curiosity she felt with off-handed friendliness, "don't get up. It's way too hot for unnecessary effort."

"Nice to meet you, Adeline, Langley." A youngish sexagenarian stood, chuckling, and put out his hand, first to Addie, then to Langley. "I see your mama hasn't let up on the heat treatment in your honor."

"Nice to meet you, Sheriff." Langley grinned back, matching his twin in hidden curiosity as well as breeziness. "Isn't it awful? How do you stand it?"

"Well, when I'm really off duty, which is about never in this little town, I strip down some, but mainly I just roll up my sleeves, take off my tie, grin and bear it . . . and sip on a gin and tonic whenever possible. In fact, how about right now, Adeline, Langley?" He smiled and looked from one twin to another.

"Sounds terrific," Addie agreed, "gin and tonic in January, lovely," and Langley nodded gratefully.

"Mimosa, the usual?"

"Please, Brice. Did you see my new friend?" Fitz was sitting by Mimi's chair, pink tongue lolling, but his ears perked listening to the conversation.

"I was wondering when I'd be introduced." Brice bent down and Fitz put up a paw to shake. "What's your name, sir?"

"His name is Fitzgerald for F. Scott," Addie answered for her pet. "I carefully named him three syllables just like the breeder's booklet said. It's to distinguish the dog-name from, 'no' and 'sit.' And, then, I immediately started calling him Fitz, but he manages." She smiled down at the little dog who was thumping a question on the floor with a slow-moving tail.

"That's you in a nutshell, Addie, careful and careless all in one," Langley teased, shaking his head and dodging her fist aimed playfully at his bicep.

"Maybe just nicely casual," Brice said. "I'll get those drinks," he added, and, giving Fitz a pat, headed for the kitchen.

"Let me help." Langley, Fitz trailing behind with unerring canine wisdom, quickly crossed the threshold and joined Brice.

Adeline meandered across the room, touching the desk and, stopping to smell its vase of stock, settled down into a comfortable chair, which faced Mimi's and matched its blue. The two chairs bracketed the large window, which framed the rapidly blackening night. Mimi half-stood and adjusted the blinds to shut out the dark and any little breath of cold air.

From her seat, Addie could see directly into the kitchen and she watched the two men intently. Already she liked Brice's casual friendly manner, and, now, she began to assess his dark good looks. Tan from working outside so much, she thought, a little paunchy in the belly, but looks strong.

Mimi hadn't spoken and she watched her daughter as intently as Addie watched Brice. "He's nice, don't you think?" She asked finally.

"Yes," answered Addie, "easy to be around, and I like his face. He looks kind."

"He is, Adeline, and a big help to me. He can fix anything and this old house . . .," Mimi trailed off.

Addie watched as the men sliced limes at the sink and plunked ice into three glasses. She could smell the perfume of the gin mixing with the citrus fragrance of the fruit as each glass received a double jigger and the tonic fizzed on top.

"I hear he's a good dancer, too," Addie said, brushing her hand through her dark bangs and looking again at her mother, her arching eyebrows flavoring her comment.

"Oh, yes, he really is," Mimi, oblivious to Addie's

Winter Goldfinch

gentle teasing, agreed and began to explain. Leaning forward in her chair, Mimi brushed at her own hair. "I had met him once, briefly, but I really met him when your Aunt Jewell talked me into going to Tootsie Barnes's son's wedding reception. He married Brice's niece, Cherry Darden. Brice's brother is a veterinarian, and he took over the practice when Dr. Hoyt retired."

"Oh, thank-you, dear." Mimi accepted a small delicate glass from Brice. "I allow myself one glass of sherry, now, before dinner. I used to have trouble, you know, but, when your daddy died, I just stopped even wanting to drink anything alcoholic. This hardly counts, does it? Well, cheers to us all...together once again. I have missed you."

Addie drank slowly from her icy glass and felt her face flush . . . with shame, she thought. This was not the mother she had expected. The crazy hothouse and nutty clothes, yes, she thought, but not this quiet little lady speaking frankly of past weakness. And, yes, accepting my dog . . . even before I threatened to move to a motel. She really has missed us, she thought to herself. As much to cover her confusion as for any immediate need, Addie rose from her chair and placed her glass carefully in the ashtray on a little side table, pulling her damp shirt away from the wet small of her back with both hands. "May I give Fitz some water and his food on the floor in the kitchen? His bowls are in my suitcase."

"There's a tray there on the counter. Why don't you put the bowls on that so water won't get on the floor, Addie? And there's cut cheese in the refrigerator and crackers by the sink," Mimi added.

"I'll get them," Brice said, "you go ahead and tend to your dog."

"Thanks, Brice," Addie smiled and hurried off to her room, wondering if she could get away with lowering the thermostat another two degrees. "God, it's so hot," she said to the dim hall.

*

Jayne Davis Wall

Mrs. Slater

Six o'clock. 304 E. Jackson Avenue. Mrs. Slater turned off the overhead light in the kitchen and picked up her glass of bourbon and seven. She stuck a crumpled package of Chesterfields in the pocket of the heavy wool cardigan she'd worn all winter against the cold air that seeped under every door and around all the windows in her little house. Tugging the sweater up around her thin neck, she crossed the cracked linoleum and entered the living room, following a tamped down path worn into its old shag carpet, and switched on a small television set placed precariously on top of a TV tray, the only furniture against an otherwise bare wall.

She turned to the Channel Six news, adjusted the vol-

Winter Goldfinch

ume until it was only a quiet hum, and sat down in her accustomed seat across from the set. She reclined her rocker, her glass sloshing and spilling a little, then, balancing it on her lap, lit a cigarette. She spat out a crumb of tobacco, drew smoke deep into her lungs, and, sighing, relaxed against the comfort of the chair.

The television droned quietly but Mrs. Slater's head was turned away. Peering squinty-eyed through smoke, she looked toward her sweating living-room windows. She was watching the falling night turn the snow to ash before the total dark would make it white again. She thought about Langley.

I was glad to see him this afternoon coming up the steps, looking fifteen still. "What was it, almost thirty years ago?" Poor tyke, she remembered what a happy little boy he had been, playing with Buddy. "Lord, they were busy all the day long, from before breakfast till you had to go hunt them down in the dark catching lightning bugs at the park."

Mrs. Slater was feeling pretty good at the moment, not really drunk yet, but she was working on it. She went back to the kitchen and brought the bottle she called "her friend, Jack" into the living-room, filled her glass up to the worn gold band around the rim and set the bottle on the floor beside her chair.

When the boys were older, Buddy and four or five of his friends used to come and play cards at the house. She gathered her thoughts, trying to focus. "God, I was lonely . . . a wreck," she said to no one, holding her glass with both hands, cigarette smoke trembling around her face. They were all smoking, fifteen years old, she thought, shaking her head as if she would clear away the guilt, and I knew they were sneaking beer, but I loved that feeling of having life all around me again, loved having them light my cigarettes, laughing all the time, and saying "yes'm" and "no'm." Just their spending so much time at my house made me a pariah in this little town, and the snobs didn't know the half of it.

She chuckled at the thought and her chuckle turned into a spasm of loose coughing. She pressed her sleeve against her mouth, her body still shaking.

With her free hand, Mrs. Slater stubbed out her cigarette in the half-full ashtray perched on the arm of her chair, and, when she was quiet again, lit another one and took a gulp from her glass.

"Whoops, only half-full," she said aloud. She was used to being her own companion. She turned sideways in her chair to lift the bottle and poured her glass full again. "Pretty soon I'll go off to bed," she said, though she knew, the morning sun would find her, still in her chair, warm her, and wake her as it had nearly every day for many years, now.

"Langley changed from a happy little boy on that day they came in crying and wailing to me. I tried to help. Read them the newspaper articles that explained it all and Buddy really seemed all right, but nothing helped Langley feel better. He was grateful, yes, but nothing made him whole again. Such a beautiful kid, acted like I was his mama . . . coming to see me all the time . . . us two alone . . . bringing me bunches of flowers, goldenrod, Queen Anne's lace . . . wanting something from me . . . I couldn't help him . . . wanted to . . . but . . . Then when Buddy left school and joined the army . . . Langley was so totally bereft . . . no other word for it . . . like he had been suddenly orphaned . . . as if he were clairvoyant." Still thinking of the afternoon visit, she mumbled quietly to herself through a curtain of smoke.

Mrs. Slater's eyes closed, remembering, but her head sank to her chest. Little snoring sounds began to come from her open mouth. The fingers, which curled around her glass loosened their grip and it fell to the rug spilling bourbon on the already stained spot beside her chair. "Hell," she said and leaned over, teetering, almost losing her seat, to blot up the bourbon with a tissue from her pocket. She sloppily refilled her glass and said in a whisper, "And that was just the end . . . Buddy . . . killed in a Goddamned training accident. Seemed like the end of the world. All that emptiness inside where he had been. And all that summer Langley acting like it was his fault . . . crying and drinking so much . . . then went off to school and never came back."

Mrs. Slater balanced her glass between her knees and searched deep in both pockets again for a dry tissue. Her tears were copious and exhausting. She blew her nose with one hand, put her glass on the floor, lit another cigarette, and leaned back closing her eyes . . . "Roger in Korea . . . then Buddy . . .." Oh, God . . . .. I'm so tired, she thought.

The news droned on with the minutes and faded into an endless sitcom, and the low volume soothed her, once again into a nervous sleep of fits and starts. She opened her eyes for a second, closed them again, then remembered her cigarette just before it burned her fingers. She blinked, her eyelids fluttering . . . awake enough to place the remnant in the ashtray where it began to smolder, burning into the half-smoked Viceroy Langley had left that afternoon. Smelling the stench of the burning filter, she started once more and stubbed them both out with finality.

It was eight o'clock. She would wake around two a.m. and start the process again. Usually, she would fall into a deep slumber around four or five which would hold her in thrall until she would wake again mid-morning, groggy and un-refreshed, and trying to remember a dream that lay just at the edge of her fogged consciousness.

She leaned back again and, in a moment, gave herself up to blackness.

*

Jayne Davis Wall

Fixing Dinner

While Brice and Langley had one more drink and watched the seven o'clock news, Mimi and Addie set the table in the dining room, which was just off the kitchen opposite the den. They could hear the men talking quietly and laughing at bits of the broadcast.

"They're apparently political soul mates," Addie ventured.

"Lord knows, I hope so. I think both are rather passionate about their beliefs," Mimi answered her daughter. "Can't stand political arguments at dinnertime."

They worked in companionable silence except for the clang of Mimi's good silver and tinkle of her china and glassware.

Winter Goldfinch

"This was Mama's china and Mrs. Sims's silver," she said. Mimi touched the ornate floral border of the dishes, her fingers lingering there before she handed the plates and the silver over to Addie. "I don't use it much, the china, at least, but I thought we would be a little festive."

A little festive, Addie thought. The last time I saw this cloth must have been on a Christmas or Thanksgiving! She flipped the snowy cloth into the air and centered it on the old table that she knew had also belonged to Grandmother Sims.

"Well," Mimi blushed, as if she had read Addie's thoughts, "it's still the season until Old Christmas, though, for once, I've taken the greenery down before. I don't know why it all dried out so quickly this year."

"I can't imagine," Addie smiled.

"I don't have a tree anymore."

"I don't put one up either," Addie answered and smiled again. "Too much fuss for one person."

Mimi could hear the sadness in her daughter's voice, but she would never have spoken about what she viewed as Addie's ill-chosen and broken life. Not anymore.

Mimi was warming snap beans on top of the stove. "Do you want me to make a salad, Mimi?" Addie asked.

"Well, no, but I have tomato aspic so you could get out the mayonnaise and put lettuce on the plates before you dish it out of the mold." She gestured toward the refrigerator. "I think we're almost ready. I know this is very summery, but I felt like, since you and Langley loved this kind of food, it would be all right."

"Yep, aspic is so good." Addie had never liked it and didn't think Langley did either. They both had only picked around the edges of the stuff when they were little, but Mimi must not have noticed, apparently just following her mother's rules of menus. I've probably had to eat it about a thousand times. What's once more? Addie thought to herself as she pulled the refrigerator door open and peered inside. "Oh good, I see the ham and turkey is all sliced up. Do you want me to put it on this platter?"

"Uh huh, Brice did it when he got home. Yes, that's the one and put the butter and the salt and pepper on the table. That's for the biscuits," Mimi said pointing to a silver bread tray draped in a lacy napkin. Mimi was hurrying now. Not used to serving this way anymore, her face was beaded with perspiration and her cheeks were round dots of pink.

"Okay, that's everything. You look warm enough now, Mimi," Addie said, watching her mother for a reaction.

Mimi ignored her and began ladling snaps into a bowl. She took a hot pad from a drawer by the stove, crossed to the dining room and placed both on the table beside the waiting vegetable spoon.

Addie leaned through the den door. "Fellows," she called, "we're ready! Mimi, do you remember, when I was a teen-ager and I would come in to help and you'd always say: 'Shake up the salad dressing and set the table'?"

"Really, Addie, the dressing did need shaking," Mimi smiled. She paused, "I wasn't always right about everything," she added, her face flushed and dripping with the heat of the kitchen. She reached over the sink and tore a paper towel from the rack under the window and dabbed her face dry.

"I didn't mean that, Mimi, but I never did learn to cook," Addie answered, feeling shamed for the second time that night. She brushed her damp hair back off her forehead and leaned against the sink. "Luckily, I never really had to except for breakfast and you did coach me on that the summer before I married John."

"I remember a lot of burnt bacon your daddy wouldn't eat, but you finally got it together, didn't you?" Mimi leaned against the sink beside her daughter. She smiled remembering that last summer. "Your daddy just couldn't

Winter Goldfinch

stand that you were leaving."

"Yes," Addie said, "and you were so nice about it even though you couldn't stand the thought of my marrying a painter, either, but, Mimi, he was so good and he would have been . . . if . . . if he . . .."

"I know, Addie," Mimi said, but she was unable to move toward her daughter, as they both seemed to wish. "Brice, Langley," Mimi called abruptly, "it's getting cold."

*

Jayne Davis Wall

**Part III
Dreams**

Jayne Davis Wall

Winter Goldfinch

Sleep

Lying in bed, Langley was hot and falling in and out of a troubled sleep.

Mrs. Slater floats across a deep pool of water, her hands trailing in the depths, dragging something, he thinks.
"Where's Buddy?" He shouts from the shore, though the pool is not wide. He reaches out his hand to her.
She turns her face away. "Buddy's gone." She speaks quietly, but Langley hears her as if she has yelled to him down a long, echoing, hall.
"Yes," he says, "then, where is Langley?"

Langley opened his eyes and, sliding half upright against

his headboard, he stuffed his pillows behind his back. He stretched and yawned, sleepy still, but awake. He hadn't dreamed about that day for a long time. He hadn't wanted to remember and he had forced it back each time it popped into his conscious mind.

Now that Buddy was gone, no one knew the truth about what happened, except Mrs. Slater. They had both run crying into her house and she had patted them and hugged them both and kept their secret, telling them that it was all right, telling them that it wasn't really their fault. Buddy had believed her, and Langley had tried but failed, and all his life had felt the guilt. Even afterwards when she had read the newspaper account of what they called the freak accident to them, the article that blamed the whole horror on heart attack, the dull heaviness stayed with him and damped him down until he felt himself just sliding along in his life like one of those mechanical ducks he used to try to shoot at a booth at the county fair. No ups. No downs. Just here and, then, there.

Why have I carried it all these years? I was just a little boy. We hadn't meant to do any harm.

Langley put his arms behind his head and closed his eyes picturing the day with its heat and fragrance.

*

Winter Goldfinch

The Holes

"Hey, les' sneak up on ole man Godley and look at his goats." Buddy's bright crew cut bobs up and down in the sun as he and Langley pedal hard up the hill that leads to the pinewoods beyond the park and the bench where they had met that morning. "Beat you," he adds, panting now, at the top of the hill.

"Don't care. Wasn't even racing, really." Langley pulls up beside him, laughing. "You think you're so hot, but you're s'not."

"If I'm s'not, you're a big ole green bugga," Buddy answers, laughing back. They are friends.

The boys are wearing their bathing suits. They are going to the pool at the park later that day and already the morning has grown unpleasantly hot and muggy, the heavy air pressing on them like wet cotton. Their almost twin striped tee shirts are damp and sticking to their brown backs.

"Les' get up there in the shade and make a plan," Buddy added. "First, we got to hide our bikes."

"What if he catches us, though? 'Member when he shot at us?" Langley shrugs out of his shirt, pulling it over his head as they wheel their bicycles farther along the sandy path into the woods, and wipes his face with it. He stuffs it half into the top of his trunks.

"I ain't scared. Was only a BB gun, anyway. And we can run fast as anything. He can't catch us," Buddy boasts.

Langley pauses. The hot air settles on his bare shoulders, a blanket of heat.

He considers his options. He doesn't want to be a chicken, but, as much as he loves playing with his cap pistols, real guns scare him.

"Mimi says a BB gun can put your eye right out," Langley said. "Besides, who wants to look at those old goats, anyway?"

"Scaredy cat, scaredy cat, Mama's little baby. Come on, Langley, please, les' just do it. The pool won't even open till this afternoon. Come on. We can go by the holes, too, and see if we see any snakes."

"You the one so crazy about snakes, but okay. We could circle around from there. We can sneak up real close from that side because of all the bushes. Just for a minute, though." Langley gives in, but a chill runs through his body and, leaning his bike against his legs, he struggles back into his shirt. "It's almost cold in this shade."

"You just wet. That's why. Langley, we got to count the goats to prove to Cordon we really went, okay?"

"Did he say how many he counted?" Langley asked.

"Uh-uh, he'll tell us if we're right when we tell him."

Buddy's freckled face is earnest. His bright blue eyes

Winter Goldfinch

shine with native honesty.

Langley laughs. "I give up. Les' go."

"There's a good place to hide our bikes. Right there. No, over there," Buddy corrects Langley when his friend turns his head toward the deep woods on the left side of the path. "See, under all that honeysuckle. Smells good, too." Buddy steps gingerly through the grass on the edge of the path. He pushes his bike through a tangle of vines hanging from a fallen pine tree and lays the frame against the tree trunk, pulling the trembling green tendrils back in front. Admiring his work, Buddy says, "Can't even see it. You can go to the other side for yours."

"There's poison ivy, though." Langley wishes he'd spotted the hiding place first and taken the good side.

"It ain't poison ivy. You know it's Virginia creeper." Buddy comes back to the path, wading through the ankle-deep ground cover.

"I bet there's poison ivy in there, too. Hope I don't get it." But Langley wades through and lays his bike against the farther side of the trunk, re-arranges the green curtain dotted with sweet white flowers hotly fragrant in this sunny spot on the path. He plucks one, removes its sepal and, sucking sweetness from the flower stem, picks his way slowly, standing on one foot at a time, through the dense vines covering the sandy soil. "Ouch!" Langley hits something sharp buried beneath the creepers. He hops onto his uninjured foot, landing teetering on the edge of the path.

Langley bends down to observe his toe, brushing dirt and broken pine needles out of the bleeding cut while he holds his foot with his other hand, balancing on his good foot and the heel of his hurt one.

"Does it hurt, Langley?" Buddy's face pales under his tan.

"Nah."

"It's not bleeding very much, is it?"

"Uh-uh." Langley is being brave, but, indeed, the idea

of hurting himself has always frightened him and just now he feels the hair on his arms and neck stand up in alarm. Ouch, ouch, ouch, he says silently. "I'm okay," he says out loud. "I just had a tetanus shot, and I don't think it was a nail, anyway."

The two boys start down the path again, but Langley stops to look back. "We need to remember where our bikes are. Don't les' forget that big ole broken tree across the path from the honeysuckle. You don't reckon anybody saw us, do you?"

"Nah, les' get going." Buddy starts walking with purpose up the sandy trail through the cool shade of the pines into the enclosing trees, which now cover the path and floor of the straight tall wood with pine needles. Here, there is no more honeysuckle or Virginia creeper—or poison ivy, only an occasional trumpet vine racing to the top of a high tree and screaming orange into the clear blue sky.

Langley trudges along behind Buddy, favoring his newly bloodied toe by walking on his heel and swinging his arms, his fingers stretched out straight to help his balance. "Wait up. I can't go that fast."

Blue jays are raucous overhead, alarmed at these small intruders. Langley feels the intrusion, and a guilty shiver runs across his thin shoulders, as if he were treading on sacred, forbidden ground, though he would not have been able to say so.

*

Winter Goldfinch

The Dream

The house was quiet save for the soft, comfortable drone of the fan she had directed toward her bed, but outside an insistent drip, drip, drip had begun again. Addie sat up and, holding the slats of the blind apart, peered out into the night. There was no moon, but light from somebody's room, Langley's or Brice's, was illuminating the snow-covered yard. The light reflected off a slight shine that hadn't been there before. "A thaw," Addie thought, a little disappointed.

She lay down again, after a day of surprises, too tired to concentrate on Mimi, who seemed to her to be as goofy as she always had been, but no worse. She'd never been anybody's idea of a conventional mommy. So she sold all her furniture and took in a handsome boarder, so what? All that dread for nothing . . . so like me.

Addie closed her eyes and drifted off.

She is stooping to pass under a fallen tree, which obstructs the path. John is reaching for her outstretched hand. She straightens and, arm and arm, they continue along the trail. The trees fall away to their left and rise up toward the high distant mountains on their right. Coming to a little crook in the path which skirts a lovely and unexpected meadow, they stop in awe-struck silence and watch as dozens of bluebirds dive into the sweet flowered meadow grass and then rise again and again to descend once more. There is the scent of clover and honeysuckle and the many-winged sound of insects. They smile to each other.

"Bluebird snow," says John.

When Adeline woke, her cheeks felt wet with dream-tears. "John," she said, soft, once.

"Damn it." Addie turned over, searching for a tissue on the table beside the bed. The luminous face of her little travel clock read three twenty-three. She threw off the thin cotton sheet covering her legs. "Lord, tomorrow two more degrees."

Addie closed her eyes and, without ever allowing herself to think of the lost John and the dream which had awakened her, drifted back to sleep, a light sleep at first, then, deepening into a bottomless pit of black. She didn't hear the sirens when they roared down Center Street and came to a stop not far from Mimi's slumbering house.

*

**Part IV
Nightmare**

Jayne Davis Wall

Winter Goldfinch

305 E. Jackson Street

3:00 A.M. Miss Verna McCraw woke with a start and looked at her clock. Her heart was pounding and her stomach was full of butterflies, sure signs something was wrong. She knew this. The neighborhood had become so dangerous. First one thing and then another. Strange men walking down her street at all hours and cars cruising by. Her fears started that awful night her little dog had asked to go outside to tinkle and ran straight in front of that truck.

The man didn't even stop, just drove away leaving poor Dixie lying on the grass. As always when she remembered that night, Miss Verna felt the tears start and she brushed at them with the sleeve of her nightgown.

"I just can't hardly sleep anymore," she said, gingerly sitting up in bed and slipping her feet over the side and into her slippers. "Maybe just a teeny little bit of bourbon will help . . .." She shuffled into her dining room, her blue-flowered flannel gown dragging a little in back. She used both hands to adjust the neck back toward the front and, without turning on a light, located the bottle on the sideboard. She turned toward the kitchen for a glass, and a soft glow illuminating her front windows, from across the street, stopped her. "Oh my, what in the world?" She didn't linger to investigate. Instead, she fumbled on the dark kitchen counter until she found a glass, and quickly carried both bottle and glass into her bedroom and locked her door.

Safe in her room, she turned on her bedside lamp and dialed 911.

She made her almost nightly report in a small panicky voice finding it hard to breathe, hung up the phone not waiting for the familiar answer, and poured herself precisely two fingers of bourbon. Making a face, she drank it down as if it were bad-tasting medicine.

Quick to wake, she was also quick to sleep and, in fifteen minutes, was snoring softly, oblivious to the gathering crowd of neighbors standing in front of her house.

*

Winter Goldfinch

Thaw

Addie heard Fitz's collar clinking, and, in her sleep-fogged brain, his imperative gradually became clear. "Rise and shine. Time to get up!"

When he saw her begin to stir, he put his front paws on the side rails of the high bed and wagged his tail until his entire behind was a frenzy of movement.

"Okay, okay, I'm up," she croaked.

Two years of living in the city with her dog had trained Addie to roll out of bed, throw on clothes and trudge down endless steps in her sleep, knowing the morning air would do the job of waking her. She could do it in seconds in the summer. In winter, it took her minutes.

This morning, however, disoriented by being away

from her apartment, she knocked around blindly for many minutes trying to locate her clothes. When her toes finally came in contact with the jeans she'd dropped on the floor the afternoon before, she tugged them on over the running shorts she'd slept in. She pushed her feet without socks into her boots, grabbed the turtle-neck she'd ditched with her jeans off the back of the bedroom chair and, shrugging it on over her tee shirt, fumbled on the floor for Fitz's lead. She snapped it onto the collar of the dancing dog and secured his wriggling body under her arm.

The sky was showing pink through the slats of the bedroom blinds, but inside the hall was almost black. Addie put her free hand on the wall and felt her way past the rooms where she hoped she and Fitz hadn't awakened the sleepers.

* * *

Addie put Fitz down, unsnapped his lead, and stepped down the steps of the screened porch onto the bricked patio. She drew the morning air into her startled lungs.

Now, pretty much awake, her eyes opened wide. A sea of melting snow and mud extended all the way to the riverbank.

"Oh Lord, come back Fitz!" Too late, he was standing paw deep in slush. He circled the yard in an ecstasy of good spirits. "My gosh, it must have warmed up 20 degrees over-night," Addie murmured, though her breath was puffs of white and she hugged herself and wriggled her toes, numbing in her leather boots.

She watched her dog for a while more until she thought her toes would break off and, seeing she'd have to chase Fitz to bring him in, propped the porch door open with a chair and went back into the kitchen where she found a quietly-risen Mimi and the smell of coffee and the clang

Winter Goldfinch

of pans and dishes combined into the cheerful morning kitchen cacophony of smells and sounds that Addie had almost forgotten.

"Did I wake you, Mimi?" Addie asked her mother who was already putting strips of bacon into a heavy frying pan on the stove.

"Oh, no. You know I just roll out in the morning these days." She giggled. "Since I stopped watching the Johnny Carson Show . . . and drinking and smoking along with him," she added, "I don't sleep late. Did you sleep all right?"

"I did, Mimi. Did you look outside yet?" Mimi, shook her head as she turned the softly sizzling strips. "Well, it must be 45 degrees out there and the yard is solid mud. Could I get a dishpan for Fitz's paws and a towel?" Addie, uncertain, cast her eyes around Mimi's neat kitchen. Then, bending over to look under the sink, following her mother's pointing spatula, she rattled a deep enamel pan out of its nest. "Oh, and are these towels okay to use?" She brought out a stack of worn beach towels.

"Uh-huh. They were always here for you children."

"The stack that used to be on the porch, huh?" Addie was amazed. "Forty years, Mimi?" She raised her eyebrows . . . and yet, you sold all that furniture, she thought with an emotion she could barely contain, but Mimi hadn't noticed.

"Well, not really forty years." She turned toward Addie, her eyes still on the frying bacon. "They probably came from your teen years when you always had so many girls over here, in and out of the river. I guess the porch will be a mess, too, by now?" Mimi turned back to the stove.

"It will be, Mimi, and it'll probably stay that way for awhile. Everybody will track in mud. It won't just be the dog. We could put up a sign, 'leave shoes on steps; wash paws before entering.'" Addie felt maligned unfairly.

"Oh, I suppose we'll live through it. Iona comes tomorrow." Mimi looked then at her daughter and tried a smile. She wiped her hands and began to place the browned slices of bacon to crisp on a folded paper towel. "Go get your dog and bring him in out of all that mud."

Mimi and Addie were sitting in silence still sipping coffee when Langley shuffled into the kitchen. He was squint-eyed and rumpled, walking in bare feet but dressed in jeans and a gray tee shirt. "I can smell it, but I can't see it yet. I'll need a quart of coffee before I can open my eyes." Langley sat in a kitchen chair, his elbows on the table, and picked up the cup Mimi had set for him. "Fill 'er up, please," he mumbled. "What a bunch of early risers."

Mimi poured his coffee. Addie reached over to open the refrigerator, not getting up, and brought out a can of evaporated milk. "I guess interior decorators can sleep till noon," she said. Langley grunted.

"Eggs, Langley?" Mimi half-stood, looking at her son.

"No, just some of that juice, thanks," he answered and held out his cup for more coffee. He had drunk a half-cup without noticing it held no cream and sugar. "Where's your star boarder, this morning?" Langley sat up straighter, now, pouring milk and spooning sugar into his coffee. He looked around and ran his fingers through his unruly hair.

"Well, usually he's up by now, but I think he may have gotten a call early this morning. I think I heard sirens. Did you sleep well, Langley?"

Langley paused, looking puzzled. Then he smiled and yawned. "Actually, yes, I guess I did."

* * *

Mrs. Slater was dead. That much was clear. Langley knew it the minute he opened Mimi's damp newspaper which had sat, neglected, on her front porch since late afternoon, not actually soaking in the melting ice pooling on her stoop,

Winter Goldfinch

but soaking up enough around the edges to make handling it a careful task.

The women were sitting in the den this afternoon, Mimi answering questions about Addie's old high school friends, until Langley sensed they were about to get into deeper ground and wandered off looking for something to read.

Pulling first one, then another, book from the shelves in the living room, and rejecting title after title, Langley glanced out the windows. "Aha, that's just what I want—the local rag—all the news nobody cares about."

Langley remembered his mother always reading it before she started making dinner, watching the obituaries . . . in case she needed to make a cake . . . bet she's baking all the time now, he thought and the picture of his mother's fragility came solidly into his mind.

He opened the front door, leaning out so as not to get his bare feet in the cold water on the stoop. He grabbed the paper and shook off as much water as he could from the slightly soggy bundle. Holding it away from his body, he trailed off down the hall toward his room, turning the thermostat down two degrees as he went. "Probably freeze her ass off at eighty-two degrees," Langley muttered and settled down in his chair, feet propped on his bed.

He carefully opened the folded paper and dropped the sports page along with the ads in a damp heap on his floor. A shock ran through his body. "My God! Her house, my God!" As Langley read, he glanced back and forth from the three-column picture of the little frame house engulfed in flames against a black background of bare trees and sky to the few inches of copy. There wasn't much there. "'Woman dies in fire . . . unable to save . . . accident . . . apparently burning cigarette . . . 304 E. Jackson . . . deceased . . . Mrs. Roger Morris Slater . . . husband, Roger Morris Slater . . . Korea . . . only son, Roger Morris Slater,

Jr. . . . tragedy . . . one daughter, Anne Barnes Slater Grimes of Raleigh . . ..' Everything except the funeral arrangements . . .. " Langley gritted his teeth, the muscles of his jaw bunching. Pressing his head back against the wall behind his chair, he squeezed his eyes shut until stars blotted out the imagined picture of his friend blackened and small on a stretcher and beyond help once and for all.

He knew that what he felt was not real grief. He knew that, but, like his faintly remembered dream, he felt left alone and diminishing in his mind until he knew he must have completely disappeared. He opened his eyes and placed his hands lightly on his knees. His body seemed to be floating and ethereal.

He was sad, but it was the sad that had been with him as long as he could remember . . . a sorrow that was hardly enlarged by all this. They had been comrades more than anything else, but she had been a touchstone for him, a keeper of his sorrow. She had simply accepted his sadness and made it a part of her own, and he, in turn, had kept her tucked away, a talisman of sorts. His life would be different now.

He stood up. "I might as well get it over with."

He didn't have to tell Mimi and Addie, however. When he returned to the den with the paper, Brice was sitting with his mother and sister.

Langley could tell by their sudden hush that he had been telling his family about the fire.

Addie saw the wet paper clutched to his side. "I'm sorry, Langley," she touched his hand. "I know you cared about her."

"Yes," said Langley. His face gave nothing of what he felt away. "She was a friend to me when I was young. I'm glad I saw her last week," he said stiffly and turned to Brice. "Was it really just a cigarette?"

"We're pretty sure. By the time we got there the house

was already burning way out of control, but she would have been unconscious long before that. There's a woman who has trouble sleeping across the street and she made the call. She's nosy enough to have noticed that your friend was often up late, smoking and watching television. I'm afraid it happens with some frequency . . . older people living alone and falling asleep." Brice shook his head and his hand trailed down to Fitz who was sitting alert beside him. He scratched the dog's ears.

"I wonder if Anne Barnes is here still," Addie turned to Mimi. "She was at Meredith when I was. I think she worked a year or so before she went."

"She married a Grimes boy from Raleigh, but they separated. I think she may still be in Raleigh, though." Mimi's hands covered her mouth in prayer position. "Horrible. She's all alone now. Wonder when the funeral will be and where, for that matter."

*

Jayne Davis Wall

Winter Goldfinch

**Part V
Endings, Beginnings**

Jayne Davis Wall

Winter Goldfinch

I Come to the Garden Alone

Wednesday. The weather, still unseasonably warm—if any weather in the South could be called unseasonable, as Mimi often commented—allowed them to crack open the windows of the car on the way to the church. The sky was blue, the high clouds, scudding. "You could almost pretend it was spring," Mimosa said, watching the winter sunlight flashing through the trees onto the wet, muddy front lawns. Addie glanced toward Mimi beside her in the front seat, as she snuggled into an old fur coat.
"Are you warm enough, Mimi?" she asked.
"Oh, yes. Probably, I should wear this coat all the time," Mimi answered and giggled at herself. "I'd forgotten I even had it. Your daddy gave it to me when you twins had your first birthday. You can't remember, but that was the coldest March

I've ever seen. A thaw just like this and then, bam! A tremendous storm that collapsed the roof of the Walston Big Leaf tobacco warehouse. It was so deep we couldn't get out the front door until your daddy shoveled out a path from the south side of the house facing the river where it was more protected from drifts. The winds, of course, had come from the north. Langley, is this breeze too much for you? Mimi turned toward Langley, slouched, grim, and sullen, in the back.

"No, I'm fine, Mimi," he answered, trying to cheer himself toward Mimi's chattiness, but he slumped back into his own darkness as soon as Mimi turned away.

The Methodist Church was more than half empty. They were ushered down through the thick, hushed atmosphere toward the front where Anne sat, alone, hunched into herself, but Langley stopped them midway, tapping the arm of the usher, and slid into an empty pew, beckoning his mother and sister to follow.

They huddled together, the little family group, their own losses with them, and Langley was conscious only now that such losses were not his alone. He stretched his long arm, in its newly purchased tweed jacket, along the back of the pew and enclosed both Mimi and his twin with a sense of love and relief almost foreign to his thoughts.

It seemed to Mimi that Reverend Thigpen had an awful lot to say about a woman who probably hadn't darkened the door of the church since mid-way through the Korean War. Poor woman, she thought to herself, sinking deeply into her coat and turning the lapels up around her cheeks, though the church was overheated and Addie, beside her, was fighting the urge to close her eyes. She couldn't keep herself together after her husband was killed. No more could I . . . after Lillian. There, but for the grace of God . . . Charles

Winter Goldfinch

put up with so much, the good Lord knows. Lucky not many people knew what I was up to . . . I hardly remember, myself . . . crazy and drinking so much . . . a wonder they didn't put me in a loony bin . . . going downtown naked with just this silly coat on and garters and stockings . . . Mimi could hardly stop herself from giggling and stifled her laughter only by burying her mouth into her collar and turning her escaping titter into a cough. Addie gave her one of her concerned looks and Mimi shook her head and smiled at her daughter and felt blessed, not for the first time, for Addie's ignorance. Lord . . . those high-heel shoes I had . . . then, finally I came to my senses . . . almost like waking up after a long sleep . . . and took over the children again . . . poor Charles, stuck by me and just when he could really relax . . . a heart attack . . . a man of moderation like he was and his brothers, sots, every one of them . . . Mimi shook her head . . . and he's the one that dies . . . a whole lifetime of taking care of drunkards and never a word of complaint . . . no justice in the world.

    Her thoughts interrupted by the rustling of winter clothing smelling faintly of mothballs and of the pages of hymnals turning, Mimi quickly stood up, flustered, until Addie reached over to share her book and they began to sing . . . "I come to the garden alone . . . ."

". . . and the dew is still on the roses . . . and He walks with me and He talks with me and He tells me I am his own . . . ." Addie's voice swelled into her mother's, a lump forming solidly, deep in her throat, until she could no longer get the words past. The thought of her daddy crowded out the music and wrapped her in a reverie as happy as it was sad, and she saw herself and Langley, flour on their hands and clothes and in their hair, leaning against the kitchen table watching their daddy roll out dough. A winter sun has given up to purple night outside the window, and over the river a great white moon is rising in the last light.

Langley and Addie have spent a happy Sunday afternoon with daddy peeling apples and measuring sugar, and now they watch as their father fits the crust into a pie plate.

"Where's Mimi?" Addie asks and leans over to stick her finger into the sugar canister still on the table.

"Addie, don't do that, little sugar cookie." Her daddy smiles his dark smile at her and pokes her tummy with his floury finger. "You both look like fat little snowmen," he laughs again. "Mimi's resting. She didn't feel good this morning. Now, you two, let's get the apples into the crust so we can have something really good for supper," and he dumps the cut-up apples into the crust and begins to sprinkle them with a storm of sugar and cinnamon.

Addie smiled to herself. Lord, I loved my daddy. That was simple. Then, surprised, thought, gosh, Mimi must have already been drinking, even while Lillian was still her shining light. She closed her eyes and bowed her head, mystified by the sudden knowing.

When she opened her eyes again they fell on the glowing stained-glass windows she'd loved as a child, the shepherds with their flocks, the angels in Glory, the Jesus suffering the children, and she felt their warm reds and blues streaming toward her and touching her face and hands. She stood again for the benediction to watch Anne follow her mother down the aisle through the rippling light.

*

Winter Goldfinch

Wind

Mrs. Slater had been buried on Saturday, the week before, in her family's plot under bare trees that bent and rattled in a strong west wind. The temperature during the days held warm and the sun had shone for a week.

Fitz went out each day and came in again. Addie dutifully washed and dried his paws each time.

The porch had been mopped and muddied again, more than once.

Today was Wednesday.

Addie joined Mimi at the kitchen table and poured herself a cup of coffee. "Mimi, the wind is blowing up a storm out there again and, really, the yard looks like maybe it'll dry out a little." Addie crossed her fingers in a hopeful gesture. "There's still ice, though, and icicles everywhere. It must be pretty cold at night."

"Well, yes, and it's a little early to be counting spring

chickens," Mimi said, lifting her coffee cup and wiping her saucer with a napkin, "but sometimes the whole thing just turns and we're warm on out 'till April. I hope we're on our way. Seems like the house inside is mighty cold lately, though." She pulled the sleeves of her sweater down over her wrists and fastened her top buttons, smiling at her daughter.

As she had been for the last few days, Mimi was dressed in a set of sweats under a heavy wool cardigan. She was wearing sheepskin slippers Addie remembered from her daddy and heavy hunting socks probably, she thought, borrowed from Brice.

Mimi put her hands over her ears. "Whoo—even my ears are cold." Her hands trembled a bit when she lifted her cup and coffee sloshed again into her saucer.

"Mimi, are you really shivering? You look toasty, but I can turn the heat up. I guess we really ruined your tropical paradise. Sorry. Really." Addie turned her eyes up at her mother, her head still bent over her coffee cup.

"No, no I'm warm enough. Just a little shaky this morning, and my ears and nose are a little chilly, but I'm all right. I know you children were just way too hot." She was smiling. "Spring's probably right around the corner, anyhow."

Addie leaned back in her chair, her face flushing to pink. "So you realized we changed the thermostat. I guess I knew because of your new costume. I must say you're taking all this change like a sport." Addie laughed. "Why didn't you just say something? Did you mind so much?"

Mimi said, "Brr-r," and laughed, too, showing her small white teeth. "Brice, somehow, got used to the heat and didn't seem to mind, so I just suited myself. Now, though, with you children here . . . ," Mimi trailed off, then added: "Adeline, I know Langley has to leave to go back to his job, but why don't you stay on?" Mimi seemed to want to continue but, instead, looked down at her cup. She put both hands around it and lifted it to her mouth without looking at Addie.

Addie stared at her mother. Mimi had always nagged and fussed at her plenty, but she had never asked for anything the way she seemed to be asking now.

"I can stay awhile, Mimi. We'll see." Addie jumped up to open the kitchen door for Iona. "Morning, Iona."

"Mornin', Miss Adeline, Miz Mimosa." She came chattering into the room. "It really warming up out there, but my daddy always did say we gets our biggest snow storms in March, and there's a lot of wind today."

She slipped her stocking feet into the down-at-the-heel bedroom slippers she worked in and opened the door again to hang her coat on a peg just outside on the porch over her muddy boots. "I'll mop my way out again this morning. Lord, this mud. Is Mr. Langley up yet? He sure do sleep late." She was half-way through the door when Mimi answered, "He must be making up for lost sleep, but it's time he was up. Just start down there and flush him out."

"Yes'm," Iona answered grinning back at Mimi and Addie.

*

Jayne Davis Wall

Gossamer Wings

During the night Addie fought her way out of sleep and lay for a long time staring up at the black ceiling, listening to the clock ticking and the house settling down for the night and the wind that was still blowing.
   Though she would not have called it back, the dream she had tried to escape came unbidden and she remembered the vision of her older sister. Beautiful Lillian. Lillian, both a dream and a memory . . ..

* * *

She is standing, light illuminating her bright head. Her sleek golden hair falls to her shoulders. Her neck is caressed

Winter Goldfinch

snugly by the twin strands of Mimi's choker-pearls. Falling from her slender waist is a cascade of lace and tulle. Peau de soie crosses over her breasts and meets low on her lovely back tying into a giant bow, which trails on the floor behind to become a silky train.

"It's beautiful, Mimi. It's perfect." Her voice is rich and throaty with emotion.

"It's very becoming, Lillian, and adding sleeves will make it into a gorgeous wedding dress."

"Let's get the Deb Ball over with first, Mimi."

* * *

This much was almost a memory. Then the invasion of dream.

* * *

Lillian runs a finger under the pearls and struggles to unhook them. "Help." Lillian's eyes brim with tears. "They hurt. Help, Mimi." Her face contorts and she grabs at the choker with both her hands.

Mimi wrings her hands and cries out, "I can't, I can't, Lillian!" But, she, too, grabs at the pearls. Mimi, her face a mask of clenched teeth and wide, staring eyes, with a sudden burst of strength born of frenzied despair rips them away, Lillian's arms now flailing helplessly at her sides, her beautiful head drooping in helpless submission on the stem of her slender neck.

The pearls suddenly break loose and scatter clacking and clattering onto the marble floor. "Mimi, Mimi, help me, help me!" Lillian begins to clutch at her neck, the pearls still falling and catching in the folds of her dress.

A great purple gash has opened and blood like pearls, but dark red, begins to fall, dropping splash, splash upon the white skirt and the dark floor where the drops join other drops until the volume becomes a force and Lillian and Mimi are swept away into darkness and silence.

* * *

Addie sat tensely against her pillows, her fingers tightly entwined until each knuckle glowed white in the dark room.

She tried again to remember the real night when she and Langley had been little, the night they sat quietly on the couch and watched their glamorous sister preen and pose as Daddy took pictures with the box camera that is still on the top shelf in the front hall closet.

There had been music playing and cookies and ginger ale. Mother dancing around to a record on the big Victrola. Addie could still remember the words: " . . . it was just a trip to the moon . . . on gossamer wings." It was an old song, even then, but still a favorite to Mimi and Daddy.

That night had been a real party, and, then, after a while there had been less and less of Lillian until she had faded from their lives completely.

* * *

Lillian was buried on an unexpectedly balmy afternoon in March.

Addie remembered the sky as a dome of bluest blue. A row of cherry trees stood just by the iron cemetery fence, soft as clouds, their petals falling, like snow, drifting, a benediction, over the mourners and the magnolia leaves which blanketed her sister's casket.

Mimi, her face white and crumpled, stood with her eyes squeezed tightly shut, her tears streaming down even so. She wiped at her nose and mouth with a wet ball of handkerchief and moaned softly.

Daddy stood beside her, miserable and swaying, not

Winter Goldfinch

touching Mimi. His hands gripped each other and his eyes were glued to the ground in front of his feet.

As the minister murmured the last "Amen" and people began to pass by the twins blocking their view of their parents and the waiting grave, Addie saw a mockingbird perch perkily on the lectern just outside the funeral tent. He cocked his head and flicked his wings and tail and suddenly made a dash at Addie and Langley. They felt his wings brush their heads, pushing air through their carefully combed hair. Addie turned her head and felt something soft touch her cheek.

*

… Jayne Davis Wall

7 Cents

"I've got to get back to Raleigh."

It was Sunday afternoon. Langley and Addie were eating toasted pimiento cheese sandwiches and drinking iced tea at the kitchen table with the *News and Observer* spread out between them.

"That's my ad. Pretty slick," Langley handed a section of the paper to Addie.

"You and Phelps must be doing real well. That's a nice page." Addie unfolded the paper so she could see the entire ad which pictured a beautiful room full of fine antique furniture and rich paintings with the words "Phelps and Langley Interior Design" in elegant typeface along with their Raleigh address.

Winter Goldfinch

She placed her elbows on top of the folded paper and looked up at her brother. "Where's Mimi?" And, without waiting for his answer, Addie said, "I think Brice is at his office. He's not really here much is he? Just to sleep and to eat—usually when he's doing the cooking. I don't even think there's anything going on."

She went on chatting absent-mindedly and, picking up another section of paper, riffled through it. "Between Coralee and Iona, I thought they were probably sleeping together."

Langley, raising his brows, began a toothy grin, his eyes twinkling. "Addie, Mimi's napping, and so are you. Good Lord. Brice is gay." Langley laughed with a poorly contained snort and tilted back in his chair until it was almost balanced on the two rear legs. "Dummy!"

"No!" Addie stared, open-mouthed. "I guess it really does take one to know one." She giggled then, laughing at herself. "Well, that's good then. Mimi is safe from the predatory male." She smiled again at her brother. "He's so nice that I wasn't worried, anyhow."

"Yep." Langley settled his chair on all its four legs still chuckling to himself.

"I can take you to Raleigh tomorrow," Addie offered, turning to the funnies.

"That's okay. Phelps has to look at an estate in Morehead City, and he'll pick me up on his way through. Real early in the morning, so I'll say good-bye tonight."

"Does Mimi know you're leaving?" Addie watched her twin as he fidgeted with his plate, pushing the edge down with an index finger until the crusts left from his toast slid off into his other hand.

"Lord, Langley don't you ever sit still even now? You know, I've wondered . . . ." Addie took her glass to the sink and poured tea from a glass pitcher on the drain board. With her back still turned, she continued, "you don't seem very undone about Anne Barnes' mother. I thought you'd be devastated." Addie turned back and crossed the kitchen to sit again in her chair. She watched his face and wondered if he would answer.

Langley looked as if he were wondering, too, but began quietly. "Well, I don't know. It just seems like nothing penetrates. It's not that I don't care. I just don't feel much of anything. Grief, or joy, for that matter." Langley shuffled his feet and plopped his elbows on the table.

He laced his fingers together and made a hammock for his chin. "Even when Daddy died, it all seemed like just more numbness set in. It was like seeing myself in a dream." He took a swallow from the melted ice in his glass. "Her dying, too, is just more of the same way I always seem to feel."

Addie looked down at her hands. "I don't feel much either. When John and the baby died in the crash and I survived, I felt like a ghost, like there was nothing of me at all, nothing . . . like I could float away. Maybe it's genetic." She saw she was tearing the newspaper into slender strips and jerked her hands off the table securing the fingers of both under her thighs. "My therapist says I'm too thin-skinned, that somehow Mimi took my joy by not understanding that I was different from you and from her, so that I never feel secure enough to allow my feelings to surface. It wasn't that I didn't have that unconditional love they talk about . . . .. It was just . . . I don't know . . . ..

"What was it with Mimi and us, anyway?" Addie snatched her fingers back to the tabletop and laced them firmly together. "Damn it.

"I felt like she had her foot on my neck all the time while her mind wandered off somewhere away from us."

"She didn't bother me quite so much. I had my own problems." Langley frowned looking toward the kitchen window then back at his sister's waiting gaze. "You were

Winter Goldfinch

always engaged in some kind of battle, but you managed to grow up anyway." He grinned. "I never saw you give an inch and, anyhow, I think her drinking was the real problem, you know."

"Yeah, I guess, but knowing that didn't keep me from spending a lot of time thinking up ways to make her disappear."

Addie was silent thinking for a moment and then she anchored her elbows on the table. She combed her fingers through her dark hair and dropped her chin into her open palms, sighing. "I never felt a single sentence I ever said to Mimi made sense to her. She would just roll her eyes or say something sarcastic. Sometimes she'd just say, 'uh huh', and I finally stopped listening to her, too." Addie took a swallow from her glass, picked up her napkin to blot her mouth. Her face suddenly changed, lightening. She giggled. "Remember the ribbon and the bulb?"

"If I didn't, I've heard that story often enough. A quarter bought a lot back then."

"I know Mimi loved you, Addie, but you really got in trouble that day." Langley took up the front section of the paper and began to rattle through it, skimming the headlines. Addie was quiet, remembering.

* * *

It is a warm Saturday in late spring. Addie and Langley are five years old. They are in the old Chevrolet parked downtown on Center Street.

Daddy has gone to the First National Bank and to Carter's Music store, but Mimi is sitting in the car watching all the Saturday people.

The noise of cars passing on the street mingles with that of the high rattling wagons pulled by long-legged mules. People from the farms in the county around the city of Windley throng the sidewalks. The whole town is rich with women in dresses made from calico yardage and flour sacks and men in overalls and crushed felt hats. Stair-steps of children, some without shoes, skirt a blind man selling pencils from a blanket on the steps of the courthouse.

Daddy has parked in front of McClellan's Five and Dime.

Mimi sits silent and still, watching the people passing.

Addie is bouncing up and down on the back seat, dying to go to the basement of the dime store to look at the tank full of goldfish. It is the most beautiful thing she's ever seen and she thirsts for the sight of it. She is like her mother only in this one trait, her desire to feast her eyes.

Langley is spitting on the window and drawing in it with his finger. "Stop it Langley." Addie hits him in the arm and he hits her back. "Ouch, I'm telling! Mimi!"

Mimi looks back over her shoulder, frowning, and swats at Addie. Addie jumps against the car door out of her mother's reach.

"Well, Mimi, look what he did."

"Oh, children, behave. Look at all these folks." Mimi invites them.

"Uh-huh," Addie, unimpressed, answers fiddling with the rope hanging behind the front seat.

Langley has rolled his window all the way down and his head is hanging out. His face is turned toward the rear of the car and his tongue is stuck out, wagging, at the passing people.

"Please, Mimi, can't we go in the store? Please, please, please." Addie bounces with each word, pursing her lips and drawing her brows together in supplication. "I just want to see the fish. Please. You said we could if we were good at lunch. Please. Please."

"Stop whining, Addie. I don't remember your being

Winter Goldfinch

especially nice at lunch, but go ahead. Hold hands and don't make me have to come get you." Mimi digs into her pocket book, opens her little coin purse and hands them both a quarter. "Here," she sighs, "remember what I said."

Langley and Addie, holding hands, tumble out of the back seat and together push open the heavy door to the dime store.

Once inside, Addie shakes loose from Langley's sticky hand and races down the steps to the store basement and the beautiful fish, leaving Langley upstairs, alone, with his quarter.

* * *

"Addie, wake-up. Where are you?" Langley tugged at his sister's sleeve and her eyes slowly turned to him and focused.

"I was just thinking that in ten minutes you made a legend out of yourself and a selfish pig out of me. I didn't feel like a real bad girl until I came out of McClellan's and saw Mimi scowling at me, and then she saw what I had in my hand and she really got mad. 'Get in this car right this minute.' She was practically yelling at me, but she had you on her lap with your little ribbon for her hair and the jonquil bulb for her garden. And . . . ," Addie emphasized the word, "you had seven cents left over. She was really mad at me and I hardly knew why. She just loved you best." Addie leaned across the table and gave Langley a gentle punch in his shoulder.

"What did you buy?" Langley was laughing. He had never thought of himself as generous.

"A giant all day sucker. It was pink and yellow." Addie rolled her eyes and laughed. "Of course, what I really wanted was a fish."

"She did bully you a lot, but you deserved it that day,

and she never really had any patience for me at all. At the same time, she tried to protect me from everything. It was always so confusing. She changed with the wind. Death, taxes and Mimi disagreeing." Langley shook his head.

"Oh, I know." Addie raised her brows and raked her fingers through her hair again. "I can hear her now, 'Oh, for heavens sake, Langley, stop that right now.' On the other hand, she loved telling about your sterling honesty and generosity. I didn't hold it against you, though." She laughed at her twin.

"Look, before I go, you must be satisfied she's okay by now." Langley watched as his sister sat back in her chair and folded her arms.

"I'm going to have to talk to Jewell, but I don't see why she's not really, and, you know, I think I may stay on awhile, anyway. I should probably give up my apartment except it's so damn cheap."

Addie had begun to feel a strange balance in her mother between a sort of stay-at-home madcap and an elderly spirit trying, on her best behavior, to mend fences, and she thought about this for a minute before continuing.

"I think she's even more impulsive than she used to be, but, when she's thinking, she's much nicer to us than before. She will need someone soon, though. Brice can't be charged with taking care of her if she gets sick or anything." Addie balled her napkin into her plate and stacked it on top of Langley's.

"You know," Addie resumed after a moment of silence, "I don't think she's said one word of criticism to me since we got home, and look how she let us turn the heat down, and I still don't believe how she gave up on Fitz. She's nicer, Langley."

"Maybe she's mellowed in her old age. Wonder what we'll have for dinner." Langley stood up, stretched and yawned. "Come on Fitz," he said to the sleeping dog, "let's

Winter Goldfinch

get a little fresh air so I can smoke a cigarette."

Addie folded the sections of the Sunday paper and stacked them into a thick, untidy pile on the kitchen table. She went to the sink carrying her plate and rinsed it along with Langley's.

Closing the door as brother and dog stepped out of the kitchen, Addie moved back to the sink. She leaned there, dangling her hands in the warm stream of water flowing from the faucet, and smiled. That was almost like having my twin back, she thought.

*

Jayne Davis Wall

Twins

"What the children have never understood," Mimi said to herself, "is what I've been through." She was lying on top of the spread in her room. "Lord knows, I've tried." A pink satin comforter was drawn up over her body to her chin, because, yes, she was still chilly.

She thought of the tiny twins. At least Langley had been tiny. Under four pounds, but Adeline was immense next to him at over six pounds. "Now, how did that happen? I never knew, but . . .." " Sighing, she closed her eyes and saw them in her mind's eye.

* * *

Winter Goldfinch

The nurse puts two bundles in her arms. Mimosa lists a little to the Addie side. "She is so heavy, and the boy is like a feather, Gertie," she says.

"It happens sometimes," Gertie Newsome answers. She is tall and plump with clear sparkling brown eyes, the baby nurse every mother in Windley wants, and Mimosa feels lucky that Gertie will be going home with the twins for awhile until Mimi is on her feet again and Mae Pearl can take over the nursing. "You know, they're fraternal twins, of course. They maybe won't be anything alike, Mimosa." She continues. "We're not going to try to nurse are we? I think we're too worn out from that long, long labor. They'll do just as well on a bottle."

"Only if you're really sure." Mimosa's blue eyes look into Gertie's and see certainty and total efficiency, and Mimosa is flooded with a sense of relief. She relaxes a little into her fat pillows and snuggles the babies close.

The sun is blinking through the bare March-wind-lashed branches of the oaks outside, and it flickers over each little head. One is blond and downy and one is dark. Mimi bows her head and kisses each baby. "So sweet," she says. "Has Charles been in today?"

"He was here this morning, but you were asleep. He said he'd be back late afternoon. Here, let me take them. Have you picked out names yet?" Gertie answers and asks and takes the babies, cooing to them. She waits at the door.

Mimosa answers, "Adeline for Charles' favorite aunt and Langley for my mother's daddy. Are they all right, do you think?"

"I like them better than something like Dan and Nan or Frankie and Flossie." She laughs down at Mimosa. "They're nice names," she continues seriously. "Well, let me go feed these chicks so they'll grow up big and strong."

* * *

But, Mimosa remembered, the twins didn't grow up big and strong. "Langley is healthy now, but he had every illness a child could have . . . except . . . not polio . . . not that . . .." She closed her eyes and snuggled into her pillows, quietly fading into a light dreamy sleep.

*

Winter Goldfinch

Mimosa Lavinia Dail

She lies full length in the grass and the moss that looks like tiny pine trees from real close up. Her chin is cradled in her dusty summer-time hands, her elbows a straight line from point to point so that her chin is almost buried in the moss forest.

She has been there a long time, her eyes tracking the progress of a line of ants, hardy forest dwellers, beating a path through the mossy green. She likes being a voyeur of this miniature universe with its velvet mounds of a different moss making hills and valleys in the forest landscape and the tiny bluets, like the little Quaker ladies they are called, crowding around the feet of the water oak that shades her in the dry heat pressure of this late August afternoon.

    Mama won't know where she is. Mimosa turns over on her back and, making binoculars with her hands, looks up through the branches at the holes of light blue, almost white sky. August is like this, the sun so bright there seems to be no color left at all. The leaves in the shade are almost black and they tremble as if some hand is shaking the branches gently but persistently.

    Mimosa doesn't want to go home just now even though her mother will be fixing supper and expecting her to set the table.

    Daddy won't be there tonight, again. It has been a month but still she expects to see him.

    She expects to hear the screen door slam and the rattle of the newspaper and smell the cigarette smoke mingle again with the salt and pepper aroma of pork chops frying and the apple-cinnamon steam rising from the open pot of just finished apple sauce.

    She misses his beery breath when he kissed her hello and especially the mornings when it was just the two of them sharing the eggs and bacon Daddy cooked early, early before he left the house and Mama got out of bed.

    In the mornings the shouting never started as it often did at suppertime when it would rise and rise until nobody could stand it anymore and everybody slammed out of the kitchen and left everybody alone.

    Mimosa stands up and slides down the bank of the creek. She is expert at this and can slip down with only her heels digging into the sand.

    The creek slips by the oak, in and out of the sand now at the end of this long dry month so that it is just a string of puddles of hot water in the sandy creek bed. She stands digging her toes into the damp sand and thinks about the shouting, wondering if there is a crawfish under the big rock by her foot. She looks at the little puddle for a

Winter Goldfinch

long time and holds her feet still until the water is still, too, and reflects the sky, whitish-gray against the white sand. All at once the water seems to tremble and there is a flash of whiter light and a great clap of thunder booms and rolls across the afternoon stillness turning it from bright white to greenish ochre to gray black in a few seconds. Now suddenly the sky becomes roiling black and gray clouds and rain races over the little girl as it begins to lash the tops of the trees and Mimosa, scrambling up the creek bank scattering sand and pebbles as her feet and hands grab at the dry earth, dashes for home.

*

Jayne Davis Wall

Winter Goldfinch

Goat Man

Langley walked, smoking, taking long slow strides. Fitz ran tail wagging, tongue hanging out, circling wide then closing around Langley and then widening again in the muddy street.

The street itself was empty in the afternoon sun, the sky a thin blue veil peeking through high cirrus clouds, but the air warm here near the water. Moist and sweet earth seemed to wait for the moment, and promise was everywhere in the gentled breeze blowing from the south across the river.

Langley hadn't wanted to talk about Mrs. Slater, and he didn't want to think about her or Buddy either. Tomorrow he would go back to his real life. Maybe a half-life, he thought, but mine. Phelps knew nothing about that day.

Only Buddy and Mrs. Slater had known, and, now, both were dead and gone just as quick as Old Man Godley had gone . . ..

* * *

There are three holes. They are deep and silent. Nothing is said to live in them except snakes. Terrible snakes that might attack you and cling like leeches until you are dead as a doornail and the weight of them drags you down, down through the murky water.

    The holes themselves are almost completely round, about 30 feet across, though one seems larger than the others, being a little distance from its companions and is said to be the deepest among them. They all have steep straight sides. Nothing grows around them, standing as they are in the deep oak and pine woods. Pine needles lie on the flat ground around them, and the still water in them is black with tannin and throws back an almost undistorted reflection of anyone brave enough to peer over the edge.

    Some people say that giant dinosaurs dying and decaying millions of years ago created pockets of nothingness deep in the earth that gradually subsided until the holes were open to the rain and the snow. Until they were full and deep.

    Some say they open to an underground river that bubbles up to the air from below.

    Whatever they are, they are frightening and irresistible to little boys, who throw rocks into them hoping to measure their depths, but, no matter how much string they have tied to each rock, no one has ever felt the slack that would say, "Yes, we have reached the bottom."

    Langley hates the holes. To him, they are only a necessary landmark. From there he can find Mr. Godley's trailer, and sneak up, or going west from the holes he can find the

Winter Goldfinch

Indian clay bank where he and Buddy and Cordon gather clay for mud balls to throw at the girls playing in Rosalie Brown's backyard. Going east they can find and follow the creek that leads them home again and to the park, which is a little south of home in a sharp crook of the river. Turning due south from the holes they can follow the zigzag line of small trees and bushes to spy on the bearded old hermit who is as scary and irresistible to the boys as the holes.

He is called Teeny Godley by their parents who had been his classmates and remembered his tiny stature even as he became a grown man, more and more a recluse until he disappeared from their view completely. He is called Old Man Godley or simply the Goat Man by most of the children.

Though none of the children really know, he is said to smell like a goat and to sleep with them in his trailer. He drinks goat's milk and eats goat meat and squirrels and anything else he can shoot. Nobody actually says he eats little children, but everybody knows that he will shoot at them or anybody else he sees on his property. The bad part is that all these woods are his. And he can catch you unawares, if you aren't careful and using your best sneaking ability.

The boys are creeping among the bushes dotted through the woods where places had inexplicably been cleared, maybe for wood, maybe for camping. The bushes, mostly young trees, really, dogwood, oak, and plum, lead very satisfactorily to a place behind a pile of earth like a small hill. The boys don't know why it is there, this manmade hill of rubble, just that, from behind it, they can peep at Mr. Godley's goat yard. Here they expect to keep hidden long enough to count his goats.

Crouched in their hiding place, Buddy and Langley are very quiet. They can hear the jays calling overhead, but the birds seem far away and an occasional bleat of a goat seems to come to them as in a dream. The truth is that their heartbeats are filling up their ears with sound, making them deaf to everything save their own fear.

"How many do you see, Langley?" Buddy asks.

"I can't tell. They keep moving around too much."

They watch the animals, black and white, brown and spotted, horned and un-horned, milling restlessly around the dirt yard where not a blade of grass grows and where several chickens scratch between their legs looking for insects in the loose soil.

"I know. You count the ones with horns, Langley, and I'll count the other ones." Buddy, on his hands and knees, begins to count silently.

"Fourteen." Langley stands up. "Let's go!"

Suddenly, from behind the torn screen door of the tumble-down trailer: "What are you boys doing? Get out of here!" He has a voice that croaks from disuse and a gun is strapped crossways over his chest. He jumps lightly over the threshold of his trailer almost losing his orange cap and starts at a run toward the boys, his face above his beard red and angry and his arms pumping, his fists balled.

Langley jerks Buddy up and gives him a push. Buddy runs to the cover of the bushes, twisting and turning among them, already imagining the sound of shots. His feet barely touch the earth. He is flying, but Langley stumbles, his sore toe opening up again and bleeding on the sand as he plows through the bushes. Langley knows Mr. Godley is close behind, almost catching hold, but after what seem like long hours to him, the bushes open suddenly and the pines close around him, and he senses escape as he spins around them and dodges over rocks and humps of roots, running for his life. He feels himself racing through the air in slow motion. He can't hear. He can't see and suddenly he is on the ground, again, pine needles sticking to his wet skin.

Winter Goldfinch

His heart stops, and he twists his body to look back knowing that death is on top of him.

What he sees, though, is not his death. He sees, instead, a tiny old man deceptively agile, trip, seeming to fly through the air, red faced, sweating and grimacing, disappear over the edge of the widest of the three holes, a silent splash in slow motion. The water, settling back upon itself, rocking a little like soup in a bowl, closes over him. Bubbles now rising to the surface, concentric rings widening, widening until each hits the edge of the hole and, starting back, collide with others still emanating from the origin of the disturbance. The body sinking slowly, slowly without resistance down to where, where? . . . until the surface is still again save for the ripples from the cap tumbling down as it fills with water and tries to sink, too, but Langley, crouching beside the hole now, his fingers and toes digging into needles and sand, grabs at it and drags it onto the bank.

He inches back and flattens his body full-length until he is lying there, staring into the black. Until his reflection looks back at him from the deep still water.

***

For a long time, Langley has known the whole story, but after the fear of being caught and blamed and being put in the electric chair left him, an enormity of guilt stuck with him just the same, as if Mr. Godley's own heavy water-soaked hands were holding his beating heart.

"We killed a man," he would say to Buddy and Buddy would say, "Least he didn't kill us, though, Langley. We didn't do nothing, really, just look at his stupid goats." And Buddy went about his life in perfect innocence until he was drawn into his own black hole and Langley was left alone in the world.

*

Jayne Davis Wall

Coffee Break

On this pale blue and windy January day, Sheriff Brice Darden was taking advantage of a slow Sunday afternoon, which seemed almost lazy after a busy week. He slid into a booth and faced his younger brother with a grin. "Dr. Franklin Darden. We're probably the only two folks in town who are always on call. Even people doctors get a day off for golf."

His brother grinned back and gave him his hand. "It's been a long time since we've managed to have lunch together. How're things going at the hot house?"

Brice laughed, shrugging out of his leather jacket, looking around the familiar diner, watering hole for the downtown cronies, before he answered. Just a few refu-

Winter Goldfinch

gees from Sunday afternoon golf, the course still half frozen in shade and soggy in sun. Male bonding continued in huddled groups at the bar over after-lunch coffee. Male shoulders hunched against the still icy air swooshing through the double doors as they opened and closed to eject late diners straggling out by ones and twos onto the chilly shaded sidewalk and hurrying to cross the street into the thready January sunshine.

The Oasis Café had been, as usual, very crowded. Dusty fronds of potted palms waved with the breeze from the coming and going; the fragrance of coffee blended with the odor of frying onions and potatoes and the clinking of silverware and glasses fused with the hum of conversation. Nice, Brice thought and brought his mind back to his brother's question, his occupational reconnoitering completed. "Well, in the first place, good news. The Manor Sims is no longer the hot house. Mimi is wearing clothes again and all's well with the world. Her children are visiting." He paused, thoughtful. "She's pretty happy, I think, but somehow subdued, on her best behavior. I haven't been home much, of course." Brice stopped, suddenly shy, and watched his brother as he stirred milk into his coffee. "Are you ready to order? I'm talking too much."

"Yeah, hamburger and fries. No, you're not. Since Cherry moved out I've been starved for chitchat and gossip. What're the kids like? Marcie!" He summoned the waitress, who took a last deep drag and ground out her cigarette in the ashtray at the corner of the bar. She came over smiling, her blond good looks fresh and shiny even this late in the lunch rush.

"You two haven't been in for awhile. What is it, a sit-in? Or are you eating?"

"We're actually hoping to manage to eat an entire meal before somebody finds us, so rush us two hamburgers with fries on the well and onion rings on the medium rare. Coffee for the sheriff here." Franklin smiled up into the glare of her great blue eyes. "Please," he added.

"Gotcha," she turned, tore their order from her sales book and swished away.

"Just needs ears and a bunny tail," Brice smiled. "You must get here more than I do."

"Nah, I usually go on home for a sandwich, but she's a friend of Cherry's. Back to our gossip. What are the kids like?

"They're nice kids, really. They're twins you know, but nothing alike. He's tall and lanky, reserved, but easygoing at the same time. He's almost certainly gay, and his business partner is probably his partner, if you catch my drift. They have a real successful interior decorating place in Raleigh."

Brice laughed and Franklin interrupted, "Not your type, I guess."

"Oh, please. Too young, anyhow, but he really is a nice guy.

"She's pleasant too. Lost her husband and baby a few years back. Oh, and she's crazy about her dog. You'd probably like her."

"Is it a Scottie?"

"Yeah, Fitz."

"I've actually seen them walking along the lane behind the house when I've been home for lunch. She's dark and sorta cozy looking?"

"I guess you could call her cozy." Brice nodded over his coffee cup, laughing.

"I've been playing at a secret crush on her. She looks familiar, somehow, as if I've known her or seen her somewhere. I even thought of walking Andrew and accidentally running into her." Franklin laughed, but his face, a younger version of Brice's, became crimson. He brushed his dark hair off his almost unlined forehead and picked up his nap-

Winter Goldfinch

kin, fiddling it with both hands until he flipped it open and dropped it in his lap. His quiet eyes creased at the corners as he ducked his head and then met his brother's calculating stare. "Well, I'm embarrassed," Franklin grinned as his face paled again with confession leaving only his ears blushing.

"Well, hell," said Brice and picked up his napkin. "I never even thought of it, but, of course. I think I might be able to put you two together. Maybe dinner or something like that. And speaking of food, here it is." He smiled up at Marcie and winked at his brother.

*

Jayne Davis Wall

Long Night's Journey into Day

"Once, when Addie and I were seven or so, I guess, there was a huge wonderful snow. Seems like it was in March. Completely unexpected. Snow. We loved it. We wanted to keep it for always."

Phelps and Langley had returned from Morehead City and were slouched on their pink leather loveseat, relaxing among fat purple pillows. Their faces were shadowed by the faint light shed from the delicate ebony lamps on end tables beside each of them. Their heads rested on the back of the couch. Their feet, without shoes now, were propped on a long, low satiny black Chinese bench beside a half full bottle of Asti Spumante. Outside they could hear the wind, and the windows rattled quietly with each new blast.

Winter Goldfinch

"You can't imagine how grand we thought it was, your being raised in Connecticut, and all. We wanted Daddy to put all these snowballs we made in the freezer so we'd always have them."

Phelps smiled and poured their glasses full. "Here's to snow. We've had enough this year, though, and, after tonight, I never want to see ice again."

"That was just it. Daddy told us the snowballs would just turn into ice in the refrigerator, so Addie and I found some chickweed, flourishing and already lush and green, under some bushes in the side yard. We carefully cushioned the snowballs and covered them with pine straw and torn-up chickweed. We were certain they'd keep, and, for days, they did. Until we forgot about them." Langley smiled a sad smile, put his glass down and began rolling up the sleeves of his plaid shirt.

"It is a little bit warm, or is it just the wine?" Phelps, laughing, shrugged out of his heavy sweater, tousling his sandy hair and dislodging his glasses. "You look sad, but, the way I see it—we're here and we're alive, unlike your snowballs."

"Yeah, I know. It's made me think is all. Addie and I remembered, finally, and looked for the snow while we were hunting Easter eggs that year, but, of course, the snowballs were gone. I think my childhood was a little like the snow. Treasured, but melted away without a trace." Langley stretched and took a long, thirsty drink.

"What the hell are you talking about? We're supposed to be celebrating. When the van hit that skid, and I saw the headlights sweep over that damn rock quarry and we banged into that guard rail, I thought we were dead for sure." Phelps gave a shudder and poured out the rest of the wine into their glasses. "I'll get another."

Langley followed him into the kitchen. "There's one more in the fridge, I think. On the top shelf at the back."

Halfway into the second bottle of wine, they began to dissect their frightening near miss.

They had finished their business in Morehead and decided to wander leisurely by back roads home to Raleigh from the coast.

The farmland, coated in snow, still glimmered pink in the setting sun. They both loved these country drives whenever they had the time, but they enjoyed the beach, too, and they had lingered far too long over their lunch on the pier overlooking the winter ocean, and the day turned into night before they got home. With the night falling, what had looked only like shallow pools of wet on the pavement became, first, slush and then, ice.

It was a patch of this ice, as the road curved around the old rock quarry, that almost plunged them into what they both thought would be their deaths in this abandoned place just west of Windley County, still an hour away from Raleigh.

Langley knew the place at once. He and his friends had visited it many times, flirting with the danger of its menacing depths. They walked around its margin, frequently, climbing over rocks and pretending to push each other over the edge.

His knees became jelly and he couldn't speak as the van jerked to a stop against the guardrail already bent when he was a boy. The headlights illuminated the jagged expanse of water and the steep banks of what he knew to be red clay, though they shone back gray in the car lights. He hadn't spoken and he wouldn't tell Phelps, who was white and shaking, his teeth chattering like castanets, but Langley knew that the stories of cars going through the same rail and sinking out of sight were true enough. True enough to remind him of the other bottomless pool. "Was this to be my punishment? How fitting." Shaking now, uncontrol-

Winter Goldfinch

lably, he spoke silently, but, in his head, heard a quiet voice. "You've been punished enough," it whispered and repeated again and again until he recognized Mrs. Slater, and a warmth began to seep into his heart. "Maybe," he thought. "Maybe." Maybe, he could tell Phelps now and later, safe at home, warm and drowsy after much wine, he did tell Phelps. He told him quietly, emphatically, and sadly, but with a little thrill of hope, at last.

In the morning, Langley stretched his long arms and legs and kicked the jumbled bedclothes off his feet. Coffee was scenting the air, and bacon, and Phelps was whistling and clattering in the kitchen making their special California omelette. Sunday morning breakfast. Even though it was Tuesday. Phelps feeling still like celebrating.

Langley's head was pounding and his eyes were clogged with sleep, but, when he opened the blinds over their breakfast nook, he saw sun and glistening pine needles brushing the windows and, for the first time he could remember, he felt almost happy, as if a balm was settling sweetly over his life.

*

Jayne Davis Wall

Winter Goldfinch

**Part VI
Aunt Jewell**

Jayne Davis Wall

Winter Goldfinch

Jewell Tells Almost All

"You know Jewell has been wanting you to see how she's fixed up her house," Mimi said to Addie, who was just getting up from lunch at the kitchen table. "Let me do the dishes now, and you and Fitz walk on over there. Jewell's been here three times already." Mimi rose and made shooing motions with her napkin, then balled it up and dropped it in the trash. "But take this out when you go. It's full." She scraped her plate and leaned toward the sink. Turning on the water and squirting soap into one side, she looked back at Addie who was still silent. "Go on now. When I finish, I'll lie down for awhile."

Addie rested her chin in her hand and watched her mother. "Mimi, are you sure? I can see your hands shaking from here. Let me finish the dishes and then I'll go while you're napping." Addie stood, hesitating, and pushed her chair up to the table scraping it on the linoleum.

"Oh, for heaven's sake, pick up your chair and stop making that awful noise. I'm fine. If you'd just leave me alone for a minute. Go on now. It'll do us both good." She smiled then and Addie knew it was useless to worry about Mimi.

"I guess you're the doctor since you won't go to a real one. But, okay, come on Fitz. Let's go see Aunt Jewell."

"Good. Put on a coat and give my love to Jewell." Mimi, leaning against the sink, watched her daughter, followed by her little dark shadow, slam through the kitchen door. The rising tide of steaming water spilling over into the empty side of the sink gurgled down the drain, and she turned to see all the soapsuds tumbling, useless, after the lost water. "Nuts," she sighed and leaned on one hand as she turned both the taps off with the other.

* * *

Maybe Jewell is napping and we can go home, Addie mused as she and Fitz wandered along Trent Lane. The lane was quiet as usual and somehow soothing as if time had slowed to a crawl there. The air seemed still for once, too, but the sky was the flat white of winter, and the leaves of the wax myrtles and yaupons, which grew everywhere along the verges of the roads and lanes in this part of the county, clicked and clacked with some icy breath that seemed to just skim their tops leaving Addie and Fitz unaccosted. Addie shivered inside her heavy sweater, more from the appearance of cold than the actual cold itself, though it seemed to be gathering like an approaching mist.

Jewell lived in a small brick house a mile or so up from Mimi. Like other houses on the lane, its back was turned to this little dirt road and faced, on the front side of its big square yard, a busy street which led to a public boat ramp, completed since Addie was last at home.

Addie loved Jewell's back yard and lingered there before going inside. *Chaos,* she thought as she entered, pushing open the little picketed gate, *but dear.* She smiled. The gate opened through a chin-high boxwood hedge, trimmed, Addie thought, by Jewell herself. *You wouldn't possibly pay anybody to do as bad a job as this.* She strolled up the brick walk and smiled at the little painted gnomes and mushrooms dotted everywhere among the crudely trimmed topiary rabbits and turtles. Tilting birdbaths, empty in winter, staggered and leaned haphazardly beside benches. Some were concrete and some were carved from great stumps of pine trees cut down, when Jewell moved into the house, to allow sunshine for her flowerbeds. The beds were bare now, but in summer they were riotous with marigolds and zinnias, Addie remembered. Now, without them, the yard seemed a little eerie, like an enchanted garden in a storybook.

Fitz, immune to spells as usual, had discovered Addie's favorite feature and was lapping water from a small goldfish pond. "Oh gosh, I loved that, Fitz." She stepped to the edge to gaze at the fat gold and black fish lying winter-still on the pond bottom.

"Oh, Addie, yoo-hoo! Bless your heart! How nice! I saw you from the kitchen window." Jewell rushed down her steps and threw her arms around Addie.

She was a very tall and heavy woman, fighting her age with coal black hair, which was beginning to thin in back but making up for it with copious curls fringing a heavily powdered face, which, though mask-like, smiled broadly.

"I'm so glad you're here. How do you like it? I've added a lot since you were here last. I've got the most amazing fellow helping me. Sol. He's steady as the planets, even though he has a little spot of schizophrenia and talks to himself all the time. He comes by every day even when I don't need him and walks round and round in circles until I guess he's had enough and then he just goes on home." Jewell shrugged her shoulders in wonder.

"Oh, Aunt Jewell. Are you sure he's safe?" Oops, she thought, wrong about the hedge.

Addie began to wonder if the insanity was catching and looked intently at her daddy's sister who had that soft benign expression which reminded her so much of him and which brought a quick, sharp pain to her stomach.

That sweet look of happy innocence and wonder, inherited, she knew, from Grandmother Sims, belied keen observing and recording natures.

"Come in, come in. You, too, Fitz. It's getting colder isn't it?" Jewell ushered them through a screened porch filled with hanging wind chimes and nothing much else, except an old glass-topped table pushed against one side. It held a stack of newspapers and an enameled roasting pan still filled with congealed fat. "Is that from Christmas, Aunt Jewell?"

"Christmas? No-o-o, I couldn't find it at Christmas. Thanksgiving, I think. Lord. I never noticed it. I just put it there to get it out of the way and completely forgot it. Heavens!" Jewell laughed heartily and shut the door.

The kitchen felt hot after the cold outside, and seemed almost the same as always to Addie, except for its size. It was still filled with Jewell's clutter, rubber bands slipped around candlesticks, piles of unopened newspapers and hastily thumbed magazines. There were books piled everywhere, some lying open, others with newspaper articles peeping out, but the room itself was twice as big, and a large oak table stood in a windowed alcove overlooking the garden jumble.

"Well, you certainly have a lot more room." Addie

Winter Goldfinch

tried to keep the archness from leaking out, but failed.

Jewell, oblivious, answered, "Yes, I had the dining room wall knocked down so it's all one room and look." She moved through an open door toward the front part of the house. "I made the living room smaller and took part for a bedroom and added a bath. Now I can sleep downstairs. The whole upstairs is for storage, which is nice." She smiled and waved her hands as if demonstrating an empire, which, of course, she was, Addie thought.

"Gosh, Aunt Jewell, you really have changed things. I thought Mimi had changed her house, but you've got her beat."

They strolled into the living room. "Grandmother's clock looks nice," Addie lied, thinking the clock looked as if it had just swallowed something labeled "eat me" and was fast outgrowing the eight-foot ceiling.

"It just did fit. You know I can't part with things like your mother can, but she was never very sentimental. Well, come on. Let's see. This is a celebration. Let's have a little glass of something?" She was asking. Addie, glad she would be walking home and still cold even in Jewell's stuffy house, readily agreed.

They sat at the table in the kitchen sitting room. Fitz, already at home, was sleeping on a discarded sweater thrown on the worn, chintz-covered couch which stood against the wall by the door.

The warmth in the room and now in her stomach began to combine with the deep ticking of the great clock a room away, just audible above the intermittent sound of the old refrigerator cycling on and off.

Addie relaxed into the comfortable drowsy feeling, almost dreamlike, as if she could ask and be answered anything she wanted to know.

"I dreamed about Lillian," Addie said, her second glass of Chablis in front of her. Her fingers followed the cold beads of moisture as they ran down the sides of Jewell's best stemware before she took a sip. She looked at Jewell whose lipstick had left traces all around her own glass and then transferred them back to the corners of her mouth so that her face became even more clown-like despite the sadness in her eyes. A sad clown, her niece thought. The white face, the wig-like hair, the clown mouth almost, but not quite, made Addie, just a little tipsy already, laugh. "I dream about her a lot, really. I can't remember very much about her before she died, Aunt Jewell."

"No, I suppose you wouldn't. You all came so much later. Let me get us some cookies." She got up from her chair stiffly. "Hand me one of those plates out of the cabinet," she said, indicating a delicate glass corner cabinet Addie remembered from Grandmother Sims' dining room. Jewell rummaged on a shelf by the sink, pulling a package of Oreos down to the counter. She opened it, spilling some of its contents into the sink. "Darn, oh well, we don't need to eat the whole package, anyway. Now, your mother could eat a package a day and it wouldn't show."

They both laughed ruefully. They'd often complained about Mimi's ability to eat like a horse and never gain in the days when Addie, a teenager, had made her aunt into a sort of surrogate mother.

"What really happened with Lillian, Aunt Jewell?" Addie pressed as much as she felt she could, and she saw that Jewell was settling down to tell as much as Addie would ever really know about her sister.

Jewell sighed, took a cookie from the plate and placed it on the napkin in front of her. Instead of taking a bite, she raised her glass and took a tiny sip. "I always feel so sorry for your mother. There's been so much sadness in her life, really. Her own family. Her parents' divorce when she was just a little girl and, as much as she loved your daddy, my mother never accepted Mimosa because people

Winter Goldfinch

didn't back then, you know. Divorce was a scandal, and she held it against your mother. Sins of the fathers, I guess. Mimi's spirit was defiant, but she had been hurt, really, all her life by something her parents had done, and she's always felt like an outsider." Jewell paused and looked at Addie. "She let that turn her a little cold, I think, even to your daddy. Afraid, still, of the rejection she'd felt always just because of the divorce. And then her children, Lillian and you, you poor child; we worried so much about you, all alone and so much sadness. How are you doing, Addie, really?"

Jewell looked quietly at Addie and Addie, forced to switch subjects quickly, was amazed to find herself answer, "Really, Aunt Jewell, I think I get better every day. It was pretty awful at first, and, forever they'll be deep inside me, but I feel almost peaceful now. As if, somehow, someone had anointed me with some sweet, soothing oil. I'm glad I came home. I think it's helped in some way, but tell me about Lillian. Mimi never will talk about her at all."

"I'm so glad you feel better. You look as if you could be happy again. I hope so." Jewell cupped Addie's hand with her own, briefly, and began her memory of Lillian. "I'll make this short, honey. You could never really know her, now that she's gone, and there's no reason you should. It's not a happy memory for any of us who loved her.

"Anyhow. Lillian. She was an exquisite child from the minute she was born. She was pretty and sweet and happy and tremendously uncomplicated, which your mother really loved. It meant that she pretty much used her like a doll. She was so beautiful, and your mother made sure she wore the right things, did and said the right things and then she held her out in front of herself as if to say, 'You don't like me, but you can't say no to this charming creature,' and they couldn't. Everybody loved her. I don't think Lillian resented Mimosa at all. It all came so naturally to her.

"She had gone steady with the same boy since she was in high school. He was a Carter boy. His daddy owned the small grocery store on Center Street, but his mother was from an old family, you know, and Mimi totally approved.

"Oh, I guess it was about 1955. You twins were maybe eleven or twelve years old then. You hardly knew your sister, I don't suppose. She'd been so popular and busy in high school. Never at home.

"Lillian was a junior at Meredith then. He was a rising senior at Carolina, and they decided to get married, even though both parents wanted them to wait until they finished school. The war was over, of course, but Russia, we knew, had that terrible bomb, and the Iron Curtain made everybody jumpy. Well, anyhow, they planned to marry in July of 1955. Lillian and what's his name, I can never remember, persuaded their parents it was now or there might not be a tomorrow for them. Doomsday was their ticket to an early marriage. I think a lot of kids married who might have waited a year or two. They felt that bomb hanging over their heads."

Jewell paused and took a swallow from her glass.

The room was very still and quiet save for a few little yips from Fitz whose moving feet indicated he was chasing something elusive in his dream. Addie smiled at him but remained quiet and looked back at Jewell.

"Well, honey, something awful happened." She paused. Pain gathered her brows. "He was electrocuted."

"What?" Addie sat up, both hands on the table. "How? That's terrible, Aunt Jewell."

"They never knew exactly. He was working for his daddy to make a little money, you know. He had done so every summer since he had been ten years old. Well, he was just in the back storage room. I don't know the whole story, but the store lights went out suddenly and when Mr.

Winter Goldfinch

Carter went back to look, his son was sprawled on the floor not breathing.

"That night their engagement announcement ran in the paper."

"My gosh!" Addie's eyes were wide and she grabbed for her glass almost knocking it over. "How awful. Poor Lillian!"

"Yes, before that, her life was like a story, I guess, and she was devastated. This was in June, and, by July it was obvious. It wasn't just the grieving, it was like she'd stepped off of solid earth into some thick haze where she couldn't see or hear. I know now it was depression. But back then, people only talked about such nervous conditions as if they were just things in novels. Never in relation to your own folks.

"Mimosa was frantic, but all she could think to do was have Mr. Hunter at the church come and talk to Lillian. Dix Hill or anything like that was just out of the question at that time, at least to Mimosa. Such a stigma attached to it, and Mimi had had enough scandal.

"I guess Lillian did talk to him, because, by August, about the time to go back to school, she seemed to pull herself together a little, and she wanted to go back.

"Mimi and your daddy, who, I must say, was very little help through it all, wanted to keep her home, but she got Mr. Hunter to talk to them and between them they convinced Charles and Mimi to let her try." Jewell topped off their glasses before she continued and fished in her pocket for a tissue. "Do you remember Mr. Hunter?" Addie nodded. "He was so beloved at the Methodist Church."

"Yes," Addie whispered, "he was still the minister when I graduated from high school. Here," Addie said grabbing a box of Kleenex off the windowsill and pushing it toward her aunt.

"Thank you." Jewell dabbed at her nose gently. "I

think if she hadn't gone off, she might have recovered in time, but she didn't have much in the way of inner resources, you see. Her life had been completely scripted for her by your mother. It made her vulnerable to suggestion, I think."

"But still, I don't see . . ." Addie shifted in her chair and reached for a tissue for herself. Now, she realized her armpits were wet and she grappled with her heavy pullover until she had it off and draped over the back of her chair. Her hair stood electrified all over her head. The corners of Jewell's clown mouth twitched but she didn't smile and Addie, catching sight of herself in the mirror over the sideboard licked her hands and smoothed her hair until it was almost tame again.

Addie was still thinking of Lillian. "I can understand all that, but how that all led to the way she died, I just can't see . . . ."

"Nobody can, really. She dropped out of school and disappeared for awhile. Then she wrote from New York. Said she was modeling, but wouldn't give her address. She never came home but once. On the bus. She was skin and bones. It was the modeling, she said. We never knew. She took off again, and the next thing we knew, she had been found dead. We don't know if it was drugs or alcohol or what she was involved in. As I said, she just went off the deep end.

"At least she never changed her name so that, when they found her, they knew who she was. Her name, at least. Who she was at that point, we'll never really know." Jewell stood up. "I'm going to make us some coffee."

"Aunt Jewell, was her throat really cut? Was that the way she died?"

"Yes," her aunt answered, her back still turned to Addie. After a moment, she turned back toward her niece. "We all tried to keep it away from you twins as much as we could."

Winter Goldfinch

Addie nodded, unable to move, while her sister's history washed over her and soaked into her pores and became part of her own history. Her chin sank into her upturned palms and she closed her eyes.

Facing her niece, Jewell continued, "Your mother naturally was never the same after that. Although, I feel like she's a little more like herself now that you're home." Jewell ran water into the pot, poured it into the well of the coffee maker and measured coffee into the filter. "Do you take cream and sugar, honey? I've forgotten."

"No, thank you. Gosh. I think I really knew it all already. I just didn't know it for sure."

"You all were young, but being young, you probably saved Mimi from dwelling on it anymore than she did. You twins had your whole high school years ahead of you, and you two were certainly a handful." She paused and smiled at her niece.

"I just happened to think, Addie. Lillian never changed her name, and you took your maiden name back after the terrible wreck, didn't you?"

The coffee pot burbled and Jewell reached up, rattling the cups and saucers out of the cupboard, while she waited for the pot to finish brewing and buzz.

Addie, her chin still resting in her hands, was sunk in thought, trying to draw some parallel between herself and her sister. "Maybe we both tried to hold onto who we were. I don't know. It's just that, when I left here, I was Addie Sims, so I still had things like my American driver's license and library card in my old name. Maybe it was just the line of least resistance and not a symbol of a new start. It certainly didn't seem like a new start. I was still a mess.

"I hadn't realized how much better I feel now 'till you asked." Addie smiled and got up to receive her cup. Fitz yawned and stretched and hopped off the couch. She let him through the porch and out into the yard.

"Watch your shoes when you go out," she said, coming back into the kitchen, "Aunt Jewell." She smiled and gave her aunt a hug.

Addie stayed just a while longer to drink her coffee and eat a few Oreos. She and Fitz were halfway home in the cold afternoon air before Addie realized she'd never asked Jewell what she thought about her mother.

*

Winter Goldfinch

**Part VII
February**

Jayne Davis Wall

Puppy Love and Pimiento Cheese Sandwiches

January turned gradually mild. Fifty-degree days became the norm. Folks without their coats ventured into the sunshine and hoped for real spring. The days were blue and gold. The only clouds were high cirrus filled with ice for somebody else.

Addie had been to share an early, very early, she thought, lunch with Jewell and Coralee and Alma, Coralee's companion. Mimi was feeling a little "pekid" and stayed at home.

Fitz and Addie had walked up to Jewell's and were strolling home again, enjoying the air and the feeling that the earth was moving beneath their feet just as the birds were moving and chattering in the trees and bushes which

seemed to gather, friendly, around them.
　These ladies start drinking too early in the day. She smiled as she thought of her tippling aunts, their cheeks getting rosy and their voices rising in pitch as they sat with their, "just one more tiny glass," their elbows among the handsome Haviland plates and cups and saucers littering the old table cloth Jewell had washed and ironed for the occasion.
　It was the pimiento cheese sandwiches, their crusts trimmed and stuffed into a plastic bread bag on the kitchen sink that led to a story her Aunt Jewell thought hilarious, her Aunt Coralee thought outrageous, and, Addie, herself, viewed with a confusion of emotion, love, joy, and, yes, recognition. "The barefoot bird lady of the Piggly Wiggly," she said and shook her head.
　"That looks like about a pound of crust over there, Jewell. You're not going to throw it out, are you?" Coralee, always keenly observant of other people's environment, had spotted the plastic bag lying in the clutter of lettuce, slices of cucumber peels, a mayonnaise jar, crumpled paper towels, and pickle jars—bread and butter and dill—on the uncleared sink.
　"Well, I am going to throw it out, but just out in the bird feeders. I don't like to, really, because a lot ends up on the ground and sometimes dogs and cats come in for it, poor things. And then they get after the birds. I don't like that, of course, but better that than what Mimi did right around Christmastime." Jewell leaned back and laughed so heartily that tears came to her eyes. She pressed her napkin to her mouth smothering her laughter.
　Coralee primly pursed her lips, though her eyes twinkled. They were all four warmed by their wine and a little tittery. "You may think it was funny, but the whole town was talking about it. Out in her bedroom slippers. The idea."

Jewell was really laughing now.

"Tell, Aunt Jewell." Addie didn't know whether to laugh or to cover her ears.

"Wait. Let me go to the bathroom, first, before I flood the kitchen. Pour us some wine, Cora."

When Jewell returned, the glasses were filled and Coralee was reared back in her chair, her hands clasping her napkin, and resting on her mountainous belly which stressed her navy blue stretch pants to, what looked like to Addie, their fullest extent. She pulled her Windley County Hospital sweatshirt down and patted her tummy, waiting for Jewell to start her story.

"You weren't here, then, Addie, but it was really cold all through December and everything was frozen, even almost all the way across the river. I guess it was cold in New York, too?" She looked at Addie. Addie nodded. "Anyhow, Mimi had been up really early, making pimiento sandwiches, for, I don't know, something at the church, I think. Brice wasn't up yet, but he was going to deliver them to the church for her. Mimi planned to make him a good breakfast since he was going in to work a little later than usual." She paused to think and took a sip of Chablis. "He had been on a case and had come in real late the night before."

"How do you know all this?" Coralee interjected, huffy.

"Mimi told me because, instead of just talking behind her back, I asked her." Jewell smiled sweetly at her sister-in-law and continued. "Anyway, she finished and wrapped up the sandwiches and, of course, put the trimmed crusts into the empty bread bags. She didn't want to put them out for the birds. She doesn't even have a fenced yard, you know," she said, looking around for assent. The women nodded. "So she was worrying about the waste of it and getting the bacon out and setting the table when she realized

Winter Goldfinch

there was no orange juice."

"Oh, God," Addie said, "I think I know what's coming."

"She was looking out the kitchen window at the frozen river when the thought struck her. The orange juice was at the Piggly Wiggly, the Piggly Wiggly parking lot was full of sea gulls, and the sea gulls must be half starved what with everything frozen and all."

"Oh, God," Addie muttered again and buried her face in her hands.

"Well, of course, driving was a dilemma. She didn't much anymore, but she didn't think that she'd forgotten how. Automatic drive and all and she knew the chains had been put on early in December. She'd watched Brice check them and drive the car out of the driveway every week or so—the battery, you know. She thought she could, but she wanted to hurry and she didn't want to wake Brice by going back through the other part of the house and changing. She had on a heavy bathrobe, already, and thick socks and those bedroom shoes that are some kind of skins turned inside out, so the fur's on the inside, you know. Well, she grabbed the bread, the keys and a hat your daddy, Addie, used to wear to empty the trash, and tramped out through the snow. Brice wouldn't have liked it, but he never knew a thing about it. She got back before he got up, safe as could be, with the orange juice, and he was none the wiser." She pushed her chair back a little. "There she was, six o'clock in the morning, dressed as she was, somewhat eccentrically, you might say. Birds flying all around her head. She said they were mighty hungry." Jewell laughed again, her double chin trembling, her lips pressed together. "I can just see it. There she was, making a myth, Mimosa, the bare-foot bird lady of the Piggly Wiggly. She didn't think it extraordinary at all, but it must have been a sight to see. You have no idea how many people are at the grocery store at six o'clock in the morning."

"The sights you see when you don't have a gun." Alma made her only contribution to the morning's conversation and hid a lady-like belch behind her napkin.

"The bare-foot bird lady of the Piggly Wiggly." Addie was still smiling and shaking her head, her hands in her jeans' pockets, when furious barking erupted all around her.

A fat black and white collie, oddly familiar, bore down on them. Fitz stood, legs spread, tail straight up, barking non-stop at the collie who was merely wagging his tail. The collie hesitated, then made a gracious bow, his front legs stretched out before him so that his hindquarters rose behind him holding his wagging tail like a flag on a nicely rounded hill.

"Fitz, stop," Addie shouted, "hush!" She knelt beside her dog, holding tightly to his collar. She grabbed the lead thrown over her shoulder before she left her aunt's house and snapped it on. "He's a good boy. Aren't you boy?"

"Andrew! Oh, God, I'm sorry. I went back in for my keys," a voice said as Addie rose to her feet. "I don't usually have him loose, I'm really sorry. I'm Franklin Darden, Brice's brother." He hurried toward her. "You must be Addie Sims." He looked stricken and his face was very red. He took his dog's collar firmly in his hand and stretched out his other to Addie.

Addie's palm was suddenly wet and memory jarred her when she noticed an old green Volvo in the driveway behind him. "Oh," she said. "Oh, yes, I'm glad to meet you. It's all right, Fitz is the one who got so undone." The dogs were nose to nose, now, wagging their tails and sniffing each other. Addie and Franklin were brought closer by their dogs and looked into each other's eyes. One set blue, one dark, and both shyly questioning. Addie felt her face flush and she said, "Oh, yes, we like Brice a lot. He helps

Winter Goldfinch

Mimi, my mother, so much. He's a nice guy."

"Well, he likes your mom, and he's lucky to have such a nice place to live. I hadn't room for him when he first moved to town. My daughter just married and moved out, but he's happy at your mom's—if you all don't mind." He blushed again.

"Oh, no, we love having him there. I think I remember he said he wanted to have you to dinner. And Cherry, is it? And her new husband." Addie looked down at the dogs. Fitz was at the end of his lead now, sniffing a bush. Franklin dropped his hand from his dog's collar and the collie joined Fitz. They both lifted their legs, scratched their disdain at whoever had been there last and turned to their people, tongues hanging out, doggy smiles on their faces.

"They'll be all right now that the formalities are over." Franklin leaned down to pat Fitz who lowered his head and wagged his tail. "I think he knows I'm a vet," he laughed.

"Yes, he is a little subdued. You must be on your way to work. I won't keep you. Come for dinner when Brice can do it, Mimi and I are hopeless." Addie waved and turned to go, feeling tongue-tied and shy, and not saying the right things. She wished she could start all over. "Well, bye." She turned back and smiled.

"Bye," he smiled in answer. "See you soon," he whispered and grabbed for Andrew's collar before the collie tried to follow his new friend off down the road.

*

Jayne Davis Wall

Cherries Jubilee

"Are you positive you don't mind this, Brice?" Addie was making a list of things they'd need at the store and, sitting across the little kitchen table from Brice, leveled her earnest gaze at the sheriff.

"Heck no. I like to cook and this recipe is dynamite. Besides, they're my folks and I want you all to get to know each other." Brice took a swallow of coffee and a last crunchy bite of his marmalade-smeared toast, patted his mouth primly with his napkin and pushed his plate away, pulling his coffee cup in front of him to take its place. "Okay. Here's what you need . . . a two or three inch . . . better make that a three or four inch sirloin steak, onions and mushrooms. Ketchup, Worcestershire sauce and but-

Winter Goldfinch

ter we have. Then stuff for a salad. Mandarin oranges and red onion, romaine and bleu cheese or feta. And, if you get some good vanilla ice cream . . . only don't get the kind with those flakes of vanilla bean all in it . . . and a can of cherry pie filling, we can have Cherries Jubilee. I think we have some brandy. I might have to look that up. Don't remember when to light the brandy. Wait a minute. Maybe it's kirsch wasser, not brandy. Cherry'll know. We always have it for her birthday celebration. Anyhow, I'll pick up whichever one we need on the way home tonight. Oh, and some Chessmen. I think that's all except some wine."

"Lord, that sounds good. My mouth is watering. I can't imagine how you cook the steak, though." Addie tapped her pencil on the table.

"You can watch, Addie. It's really easy." Brice started to get up. "Oh, and Addie, could you get some of that really good Italian bread they have at Food Lion?" Brice smiled and carefully pushed his chair under the table and began to clear his dishes.

"Don't bother with that, Brice. I'll do it. You go on and fight some crime." Addie smiled and got up from the table herself.

"Thanks, Addie. I'm hoping this wave of lawfulness lasts through Sunday, but, no matter what, I'm off all day and until midnight." Brice grinned broadly, zipped himself into his jacket and hurried out of the kitchen door.

"Brice," Addie started to say, but he was gone and the cold air rushed in making the windows all rattle until the kitchen was left in silence again save the ticking of the clock on the shelf over the stove and a distant sound of muffled coughing.

Addie stood for a long time at the sink, her hands dawdling in the water warming from the faucet as she watched the rising suds from the great squirt of Dawn she had applied with one hand while her other swished the water slowly into a lazy swirl. She began to add the few plates she and Brice had used and began automatically to wash dishes, wipe the table and counter and return the orange juice and cream carton to the refrigerator. Finally she dried her hands and bent down to feed Fitz the little corner of bacon she had saved for him. Sliding her back down against the stove, she plopped on the floor and pulled him onto her lap and began to smooth the spiky fur from over his eyes so that, shiny and black, they looked seriously and unimpeded back at her. "What are we going to do with Mimi? She can't be sleeping, coughing like that. I wish we could get her to go to a doctor."

"You two communing in a private way or can I come in the kitchen and have some breakfast?" Mimi had entered silently, walking in her Piggly Wiggly slippers. She was dressed in a baby blue sweat suit Addie had just bought for her at the Walmart store and looked tousled and rosy from sleep.

"Good morning. I'm glad you slept in. You can't be sleeping much at night." Addie stood up and took the cream and orange juice out again. "Eggs? There's bacon on the stove." She was placing a slice of bread in the toaster and reaching for the butter in the cabinet beside the kitchen window.

"No, honey. Just that toast will do me this morning. It's so late."

"Mimi, please let's make an appointment with your doctor. You probably have, at the least, bronchitis." Addie pushed her hair off her forehead and leaned against the counter waiting for the toast. The sun was beginning to slip in the window from the east illuminating one side of her face and turning her straight dark hair into a sheet of strands like alternating veins of gold and coal. Mimi, at the table, put her hand out into a slanting stream of light as if to catch and hold it.

Winter Goldfinch

"Your hair is getting longer, Addie. It looks so pretty."

"Mimi, what about the doctor?"

"Please stop worrying about me." Mimi drew her eyebrows together making a face like a petulant child. "I have this cold every winter. It finally goes away. I don't like to take medicine or go to the doctor, either, and I'm all right all day. It's just at night and I'm used to it. I don't even wake up." Mimi smiled and poured some juice. "Vitamin C. That's all I need."

"Ha. Mimi, just please don't let it go on much longer. It could be pneumonia for all you know." She buttered Mimi's toast. "Do you want some marmalade?" She placed the plate of bacon and toast in front of her mother and turned to pour coffee for them both.

Mimi shook her head. "Thanks. Now tell me about this party you and Brice are planning."

* * *

The heavy front door was sticking from disuse and the damp winter weather and Addie opened it with great difficulty so that a fine line of moisture from nervousness and effort beaded her upper lip and she felt her cheeks flame to match her soft red sweater.

"Oh, come in. Welcome. I was about to ask you to put your shoulder to it, Franklin." She accepted a bottle of burgundy from him and a little bunch of forced jonquils from Cherry. "Oh, how lovely. Both. Thank you. Too much, but, oh, how nice of you. I'm so glad you could come." Addie felt her face getting hotter and wetter by the minute as she stood under the foyer light, knowing she had just managed to make them all uncomfortable with her rush of words. Stepping back so Franklin could close the door and clutching the wine and flowers, she said, "You must be Cherry." She thought, is he tongue-tied or what? I need help here. The beautiful young girl smiled, her mouth full of pearls, and blushed. She was slight and blond with tiny little Christmas angel features and favored her father only in the smoothness of a skin ready to blush or blanch as any slight emotion played visibly over her sensitive face.

"I'm so glad you could come," Addie said again and wondered just how many times she could possibly repeat it in one single evening.

"I'm sorry, Addie. This is my daughter, Cherry. I had forgotten you hadn't met."

Addie noted the deepening red of his face and took pity. She placed the wine on a little table by the living room door and the flowers in the chair beside it. "Mimi must have overlooked these two while she was selling off our heritage." She laughed. She was used to the Spartan room now and bore no grudges. "Here, let me take your coats. I'm so sorry Wilson is out of town. When will he be back?" She hung the coats, retrieved her gifts and began to lead her guests to the den.

After food had been eaten, wine had been drunk, and the Cherries Jubilee, with its flaming brandy, had been hailed a great success, Mimi, who had seemed distracted yet smiling as the dinner swirled around her, had been urged to go off to bed. The rest of the party crowded into the kitchen over Brice's assurances that clearing up could better be accomplished without their help.

The dinner had been both convivial and rowdy. The participants were now glowing and familiar and comfortable with each other, even Cherry, who had only tasted her wine. "That was my grandmother's roast recipe, wasn't it Uncle Brice?" Cherry asked as she dried and stacked plates on the counter for Addie to put away.

"Actually," Brice began. He dried his hands and took another swallow of burgundy from his almost full glass, then plunged immediately back into the steamy suds. "It

Winter Goldfinch

was your great-grandmother's recipe. She was a good old Yankee cook and really knew how to turn out some rare beef. It looks like we all liked it." He laughed and elbowed a plate of scraps to Addie for Fitz who was bustling around underfoot and in the way.

"Come on, Fitz, out on the porch. I probably should walk him after he finishes. I don't like to let him out alone this late for fear he'll leave the yard." Addie put the plate down on the porch and stepped back into the kitchen.

"I'll go with you." Franklin, speaking more quickly than he intended, fumbled the ice cream carton he was trying to replace in the crowded freezer and dropped a can of frozen orange juice on his foot. "Ouch," he said, his face turning red as he tried to stop the rolling can before it bumped into Addie's foot.

"Got it," she said stooping to grab it. "Are you all right?"

"Thanks. Hardly wounded at all. Cherry," he said, redirecting the embarrassing conversation, "are you all right to drive home?" He knew the answer since he had watched his daughter during the evening, curious about how she reacted to Addie, and he smiled at her. "I'll just walk up the lane afterwards."

Cherry, spending the night at her father's house, was beginning to be sleepy and said her goodbyes in the warm kitchen with only a faint blush on her pretty face and many promises to come back and visit while her husband was away.

Addie and Franklin and Fitz, urged by Brice to just leave him alone, walked out into a night full of stars. The night seemed magic and breathless with waiting. The two walked, their sleeves brushing together and sending little sparks up their arms to their faces, which were red-cheeked and afraid to look anywhere except straight ahead.

For Franklin's part, he felt the future pressing on him as a dream and lifting him to heights of elation he had been denied for such a long time. He saw how easy it would be to turn to Addie and take her in his arms. When he turned toward her, however, his body intuitively recognized that imagination was out-distancing reality, and starting to turn back from impulse, he felt his hands ball into fists. He shoved them safely into his pockets. Not yet, he thought.

Addie, at the same time, felt her body receive the impulse and thought she could hear his heart beat until, smiling, she realized it was the booming of her own romping heart sounding in her ears.

When they both saw the star blaze across the sky leaving an afterglow like a disintegrating green rainbow, neither spoke, but their faces, pale, now, with the reflected light from the moon, turned toward each other in shared wonder.

*

Winter Goldfinch

Addie Dresses Up

Addie leaned her bare shoulders against the coolness of the booth. "It's warm in here." She touched her cheeks still rosy from the exertion of dancing on the crowded floor.

"I'll get us another drink. I'm hot, too. Want another G. and T.?" Franklin fanned his suit jacket against his chest and looked around for their waiter.

"No. I better have a coke this time. This is sorta a dive, isn't it? It used to be a really quiet supper club." Addie looked around, the crystal ball turning over the center of the dance floor, sparkling across her face. She watched the same effect on Franklin and felt almost dizzy. "Franklin," she said, "let's just go have coffee at Mimi's. I think there's pie."

"Thank God. This wasn't a good idea." He paused and his eyes twinkled with light caught from the turning ball. "It was worth it to see you in that dress though." He smiled and slid out of the booth to hold Addie's coat for her. She wrinkled her nose and smiled back at him. She pulled her wrap close around her and, jamming her fingers into her gloves, pushed her arm through his. Braced for the cold air, they walked quickly to the car and drove in silence to Mimi's.

Addie was curled in Mimi's blue and white chair, her bare feet tucked under her. Warm light from a lamp on the desk and spilling out of the kitchen touched softly over both their faces. "Tell me about your wife, Franklin."

His tie loosened and his suit coat draped over a kitchen chair, Franklin sat comfortably across from Addie with his feet stretched out toward her. "It seems like such a long time ago and now I guess it is, really. Ten years or so.

"We were sweethearts in high school and neither of us ever even thought about anybody else. When she finished college we got married and she helped me through vet school. She didn't really ever work at anything but little temporary jobs although she had trained as a nurse. Cherry was born so soon."

He stopped, looking at his feet, his head hanging forward, and turned sideways to look up at Adeline. His face became pinched and closed when he continued. Adeline gazed back at him and tried to keep pity out of her eyes.

"She had breast cancer when Cherry was ten. She went through all the awful stuff, but, in the end, it got her.

"When she was gone, I thought a change would help both Cherry and me and I took this practice when I saw Dr. Hoyt's ad in a veterinary journal. Been here and alone . . . gosh, it's not ten. It's twelve years now." He sighed, blushed, sat back in his chair.

Winter Goldfinch

"I'm really glad I met you." He leaned his head back and closed his eyes. "What about you, Addie?"

Addie placed her hands in her lap. Her fingers played nervously with her dress, which spread, puffy and many-layered over the chair. "John was my college sweetheart. He was a wonderful painter. He was just wonderful. I was just a mediocre watercolor gal. No, really, I was. I never would have been really good." She waved away his objections. "His family loved me, though, and they were willing to back John in practically anything, I think. They believed so much in him and let him have a small trust fund they had been saving in since they had been married. It was enough for us to get started and to live on until he started selling, and they were so sure that he would." Addie turned toward the black square of sweating window beside her, pausing a moment before she began again. "So, once he finished his B.F.A., we took off for Europe. We settled in Spain since it was so cheap back then. He painted and I worked in a little museum shop until Johnny was born." Addie stopped once more and looked at Franklin. "I don't really like to talk about the baby." She pushed her fingers through her hair and, then, clasping her hands tightly, Addie buried them in the folds of her dress again and continued with a lightness of voice she hoped would belie the emotion that began to envelop her.

"Anyhow, this one weekend in June we were coming back from Munich. We had taken a couple of weeks to tour around and to look at the university. Just for fun. We spent a few nights in Italy and were driving back along the Italian Riviera, on our way home. It's beautiful there in Italy. Hillsides all covered in grapes and fields of carnations everywhere. Little open air cafes by the road under fragrant arbors, not grapes, but something flowering, where you could get fresh pasta. The air, hot and dry, but cooled by a breeze blowing off the Mediterranean. And the wine, so wonderful."

Addie stopped again and wrinkled her brows trying to capture the memory of a day she'd never wanted to remember. "A little sports car, red." She paused again picturing it, closed her eyes and laced her fingers together, until they glowed white in the gentle light, in a determined effort to still their twisting and writhing. "It was passing on a curve coming right at us and the next thing I remember was waking up in a bright, white room, little nuns scurrying around. Tubes attached to me everywhere. No John. No baby. No anything, anymore. Strange, though." Addie stopped, thinking. She remembered something else, something she couldn't say out loud . . .. She closed her eyes, remembering. She couldn't see the crash exactly, but afterwards . . .. She could picture herself standing beside the road and, seeing it in her mind's eye, she knew it had happened that way. She could see cars screeching to stop and getting all tangled up together and John holding the baby was standing right there, close, next to her . . .. She could feel them there, but slowly she felt their presence begin to withdraw from her and dissolve.

She reached for them then, but they were gone and she could feel a terrible loneliness and the sudden sucking of black and . . .. "Yes," Addie said out loud. "And then I woke up." Addie could feel her lips quiver and the skin of her face felt plump and soft with a fullness she hadn't felt before, and tears began to course down her cheeks.

Franklin lurched to his feet and threw himself onto his knees by Addie's chair. "I'm sorry. I'm sorry. I should have realized. I shouldn't have . . .." He took her hands and put them against his face, which darkened with pain and concern. "I shouldn't have asked. Please don't cry."

And then Addie smiled, shining through her tears.

"No. You don't understand. I'm glad. I'm so glad. I thought it was all over, but I've never cried for them before,

Winter Goldfinch

not like this. I've never ever been able to. It's like a storm bursting inside me and now . . .. Oh God. After such a long drought. It feels so good. It is finally all in the past. Over. Just really over." Addie was crying and laughing now. She struggled out of her chair and pushed past Franklin into the kitchen. She tore off a handful of paper towels, blew her nose and blotted her wet cheeks and chin. "The tears just keep coming! You must think I'm crazy."

"No I don't. I'm astonished. I just don't want you to hurt. Not ever." Franklin's face eased and creased into a slight smile, and he stood up and pulled her gently against his chest and held her for a long minute. Addie smiled. Her wet face beamed .

After awhile, he said red-faced "I'm going to leave you now, though. I think you might need to be alone."

He hurried into the kitchen and put on his coat. Now a huge smile burst over his rosy face. "I think I love you a lot."

Addie smiled back at him. "Thank you for a lovely evening," she said, her eyebrows arching and, laughing aloud, she reached up to kiss him lightly with tear-damp lips.

*

Jayne Davis Wall

Dogwoods in Bloom

The morning Mimi woke, not quite knowing where she was, was gray. The sky, full of heavy, wet snow falling everywhere like marshmallows, was low and pressing on rooftops.

It was a Monday in February.

The Japanese quince was pink through the white haze and the forsythia was beginning, but there had been a sudden cold front. It came in the night from the north, freezing the brown blades of grass and the water in bird baths, freezing pipes and cracking branches beginning too early to leaf out. This front met and embraced moisture coming up from the south causing first rain, frozen as it fell, then sleet, and finally this lovely cotton ball snow.

Winter Goldfinch

The two fronts crept slowly arm in arm out toward the coast. When the sky cleared, there would be six to eight inches of white and a temperature low enough to ensure that the snow would stay for a while.

But now, it was still gray, and the sky was filled with whirling white eddies. Glorious, Addie thought. She was drinking coffee and watching through the kitchen window.

It was already ten o'clock when Mimi's absence began to tug at her. "I suppose she's just snuggling and enjoying the snow, Fitz. Let's go out for a minute and then we'll check. I heard her coughing again last night. She's not sleeping well, I'm sure, and she's been staying in bed a little late but not this late. Wish I could get her to go to a doctor. Won't be today, though. Iona sure can't make it in." Addie chattered to Fitz who paid close attention, his bright black eyes following her. He stepped, first on one foot then another, and his nails scrabbled on the linoleum.

Addie pulled her sweater over her pajamas and stepped into her boots, which she snatched into the kitchen, quickly closing the door. "Okay, let's go."

She opened the door again and they stepped into the pure frigid air of the porch. The snow came high on Fitz, almost to the top of his back, and he hopped about like a cat pouncing on an unsuspecting mouse. "Quick Fitz, I'm too cold. Hurry!"

Fitz obliged. A steaming stream made a yellow well in the pristine blanket beside the boxwood hedge which bordered the walk. Finishing with a flourish of scratching with assertive back legs, he hopped up the back steps and they both tumbled through the door into the kitchen.

Standing on the rug by the door, Fitz shook himself with energy and dropped to his back rolling, short legs flying, back and forth.

Addie stomped her boots on the rug and then kicked them through the door onto the porch. She grabbed a towel from under the sink and wiped the melting snow from the floor and gave Fitz's feet a cursory swipe. "Let's go see Mimi."

When Mimi didn't answer her quiet knock, Addie opened the door. Mimi was propped up on her pillows, looking through her windows toward her snow-covered yard.

The drapes were open for the first time since the cardinals had died.

The pink of the quince was just visible but the yellow of the forsythia was completely obscured by the falling snow.

Mimi turned to Addie. "Look," she said, her eyes wide, "the dogwoods are blooming."

*

Winter Goldfinch

Last Rites

Mimi lay in a quiet room full of white light reflecting off the windshields of many cars and the shining snow quickly turning to ice in the bright sunlight.

Through the double windows of the pleasant room, there was blue sky, and, over the parking lot and beyond the highway which snaked along the outskirts of the little city, Addie and Langley, for days, had watched the river's distant sparkle, but Mimi did not open her eyes.

When a nurse paused at the door and smiled, Addie and Langley took the hint and tiptoed out of the room and down the carpeted hallway to a tiny sitting room, which also faced the river.

No sound, none of the usual hospital clatter, no chattering nurses broke the heavy quiet. This was the terminal wing of the county hospital. Addie and Langley whispered.

"What did Dr. Lewis say this morning? I still can't see why she went down so fast." Langley asked stretching out his legs and yawning, his eyes squeezing shut and his arms over his head.

"I know you must be tired. Thanks for staying last night. I really needed the break, but I'm surprised you didn't sleep till the afternoon." Addie answered his yawn with a yawn of her own, holding her hand over her mouth. "Langley, I don't think it was really so fast. She must have been getting worse and worse every year . . . until finally her lungs are just . . . gone, useless. I think it was probably so gradual, over the years, that, maybe, she didn't even realize, herself. Anyhow, Dr. Lewis said that he couldn't tell for sure, but, probably, she'd last a week or ten days at the most. You go on back to Raleigh, though, if you need to. I'll be here." Addie shifted in her seat and sighed.

"I need about a day, and then I'll be right back to stay till the weekend, and you could always call me if you need to.

"I don't even think she knows I'm here, anyway." Langley leaned forward in his chair as if he had already started on his trip home.

"It's hard to know. I think she's in and out, but yesterday, that really nice nurse, the older one . . .." Langley nodded and sat back again in his chair, picked up the ashtray on the table beside him and slowly turned it around and around in his hands. "She asked me about what kind of mother Mimi had been, and, it was strange, what popped into my head. Not all the fights we used to have or how she didn't seem to like anything I ever did, but something else from when we were real little, maybe four or five.

"Do you remember the summer we found the Christmas lights in the garage, and she let us string them all up in that great big cedar tree in the front yard, and we pretended

Winter Goldfinch

it was Christmas morning?" Addie grinned, but the memory made her eyes fill.

"Lord, yes," Langley answered, breaking into a grin, himself. "I do remember, and we brought all our toys out in the front yard, and, then, we laid ourselves down on towels right under the tree like it was Christmas Eve. God, in August! I hadn't thought of that in forever."

"Me either, but, what I started to say was that Mimi smiled as if she were remembering it, too, so I think sometimes, at least, she knows we're with her.

"It made me wonder, though, what kind of mother she really was. When you think about the funny, silly things, she was really indulgent. Remember when we'd get mad at her and run away from home, but, really just lock ourselves in the bathroom with our blankets and a box of Ritz crackers?"

"Yeah, we were always doing that and she just laughed it off, even when we actually ran away to that vacant lot in the dark and nobody could find us for hours." Langley smiled and stood up. "I'm going to get going. Let me know if I need to come quick. It won't take more than an hour if the roads are okay." He smiled again into his sister's sad face and touched her hand. "Stiff upper lip," he added and disappeared down the quiet corridor.

Addie looked at the empty doorway feeling her heart sink in her chest. Then, she squared her shoulders, pushed her fingers through her already disarranged hair, and, tugging her sweater down over her hips, stood to go in the opposite direction, back to Mimi.

*

Mimi Floating

"Chapter One."

Mimi could hear Addie, but her voice came from a long, long way away.

She began, "It is a truth universally acknowledged that a single man in possession of a good fortune must be in want of a wife."

"However little known the feelings . . .."

Deep in the dark of a soft black velvety cocoon of selfness, Mimi thought she knew what her daughter was trying to do and laughed out loud. *Precious Adeline,* she thought. *We always connected on that, at least. Darcy . . ..* Her mind slipped away again. Back into the clamorous darkness, a darkness

Winter Goldfinch

full of fluttering and dear, almost forgotten, voices. Daddy must be close and she has seen Charles and Lillian hovering near, touching her brow like wispy tendrils of hair moved by a breeze. Charles whispered close to her ear over and over one single word that she just couldn't make out. She could feel his breath, warm and soft, touch her face.

Mama had been standing by the bed in her wedding gown. The flowers held loosely in her gloved hands scented this dark place and Mimi felt the fragrance fill up her body. *Mama, you look so beautiful in your dress. How did it turn out so bad? It was real terrible for me.*

"I know, Mimosa." A tear crept down through the powder on one cheek. "I know." Her gloved fingers brushed at it and the tear vanished.

Mimosa heard her daddy's voice and imagined his face, eyes crinkled at the corners and twinkling blue. "Do you remember, Mimosa?" His mouth appeared, corners turned up, but disembodied like the Cheshire cat. He chuckled. "Move over a little, Charlotte," and his face joined his mouth, his bald head, shiny with some reflected light, tilted toward her mother.

Remember what, Daddy?

"The coat. You begged me for it. Called me long distance from school. You promised me you would pass French that semester. You begged and promised."

I remember, Daddy. It was beautiful. I kept it until way after Addie and Langley were born and the fur began to fall out.

"You didn't pass French, though."

No, Daddy. I never did.

"Sorry to interrupt, Miss Sims. I need to check her blood gases and do her meds." Addie stood up and closed her book. "It's nice to read. Your mother can hear you perfectly, you know. There's nothing wrong with her ears." Mimosa heard a soft voice coming from the far place near Addie.

"It's okay. I need to step out a minute. I think I saw Dr. Lewis go by in the hall."

Addie smiled sadly at the brisk, quiet nurse and walked into the corridor.

Mimosa thought she could hear footsteps receding quietly as her body was turned to one side and something hard and cold was placed on her back. *No, don't leave me. Addie! Mama!*

"I'm still here, Mimosa."

"It's all right, Miss Mimosa. This won't take long. Just a little prick. It's okay, darling. Just hold on a minute." Talking all the time, the nurse went about her business quickly and gently, but Mimosa, hearing the nurse-voice echoing from the far place and feeling the cool hands on her arm, was fearful.

"Mama," she said aloud, and felt her arms being placed gently by her side and her body being covered again with the silky sheet. She slipped gratefully back into dark.

"I'm sorry, Mother." At first Mimosa thought Addie had spoken, but it was Lillian. She was all in white like her grandmother, and her bright blondness lit the space around her, holding against Charlotte's darkness, which seemed instead, to pull all other light into itself.

My beauty. You look just like you did that afternoon trying on the deb dress we wanted altered to make your wedding dress.

"I know. I'm sorry."

Mimosa, struggling in her dark, drifted away from the hurt and back again to Addie's living voice, coming once again from the far place beside her bed.

" . . . She fancied herself nervous. The business of her life was to get her daughters married; its solace was visiting and news."

Addie paused, "Chapter Two." She continued.

*

Winter Goldfinch

Answering the Question.

Addie had called Langley in the morning and, unable to reach him, left a message on his machine, so she was alone with Mimi and a sweet-faced and bespectacled nurse at her side.

In the gloom of the late afternoon, the sun slanting across the white bedclothes and Mimi's pale face, Addie, holding her mother's hand, still wanted the answer her granddaddy had asked, smiling, many times. "What's it all about? My, my, my," he'd shake his head and say, and his eyes would twinkle. His family never knew what would occasion the question. It was often simply a barking dog or a crying baby, only sometimes did it seem to have any philosophical content, but Addie, shifting beside the bed, knew her question was larger than dogs and babies. Her question fell into the third category. How to be happy. Addie had pondered this from the first time her mother had told her she'd step on her bottom lip if she didn't stop pouting. She had always tried, she thought.

John had been happy. Addie was sure of that. Their baby had been happy, too, she thought. Laughing and giggling all the time. Happy by nature, maybe.

The one who wasn't happy was Addie, herself. She had always put on a good front, especially with John, and now, here she was, without the ones, at least, she knew she had loved, watching Mimi slowly, slowly fade out of her life as well, and she was still asking the same question and still wondering. Could it be only that this static peace she had lately begun to feel was all that she had really lacked in her life?

Addie thought about how much she had tried to ignore her mother almost all her life. How could a Mimi ignored be blamed for robbing her of anything? Even this new quiet feeling of being in place and still that she'd begun to experience since coming home. Mimi hadn't loved her the way she had loved Langley. Addie had always believed this, but had she been wrong?

Mimi had seemed different this time. It was as if Addie had made it all up. As if her whole life had been in her imagination only. As if she, herself, had been the angry, niggardly one, the one holding back.

It was as though in her withdrawal she had hardly directly experienced anything from the days when she was a little girl until this minute when Mimi lay dying.

Was it only an imagined life that existed between now and that afternoon when she had felt her mother's finger, so big and safe, clutched in her own small one as they crossed that wet winter evening street with her grandmother holding her other hand? Stiff soldier boys before her and

Winter Goldfinch

behind her, their arms filled with packages, the Christmas lights and neon store signs reflecting in the icy puddles—green, red, blue, orange, and yellow. Everything between that night and this silent, snowy afternoon seemed to fall away, and she was little Addie, again, amazed and happy, her mother's little girl.

Only, this time, it was Mimi who was in the middle and a starched, rustling nurse was on her other side.

She felt the moment harden into always as she once again held Mimi's hand and saw the liquid blue of her eyes disappearing for the last time and heard the quiet sigh that did not come again.

Addie, now really alone, became truly, once and for all, her mother's little girl, and felt, at last, her mother's love flood all around her. And, in the warm room, the blue gone forever, the breath stilled, she felt her mother's feathery touch on her shoulder while the welling tears spilled out onto her cheeks and ran down her face until they wet Mimi's small white hand still clasped tightly in both of hers.

*

Funeral Meats

Everyone had gone home. The casseroles, Jell-O-salads and cakes were stored everywhere, in cabinets, on counters, some just put on the porch to keep cold. Langley, staying a few days, and Brice had both gone to bed. Iona was staying the night. They'd finish the kitchen in the morning.

It was late and Addie and Iona were having a last cup of coffee before turning in. The light in the kitchen held the cold black of night from closing in on the cozy room.

Addie's eyes were puffy and red and damp tissues surrounded a box of Kleenex on the kitchen table.

Iona sat, with her hands cupped around her mug, her rough elbows resting on the table. She was looking at her reflection in the panes of the door to the porch. "There was sho' a bunch of peoples here after that funeral," she said.

"Uh-huh, more people at the funeral, too, than I expected and more food than I know what to do with. You'll have to take a bunch of it home, Iona. I can't eat it all."

"Um'um, I will, but you keep some. I bet you be feeding Mr. Franklin ever' day now that you ain't spending all that time at the hospital." Iona grinned.

"Oh, Iona, I don't know. Maybe." Addie smiled a little and folded her arms on the table looking down into her cup and changed the subject. "You know I spent so much of my life not thinking I cared about my mother. I mean I loved her always, but she and I were so different, I guess."

"Uh-huh." Iona was musing. "My mother and me was the same way. We use to never could get along and all. My mother was real special, though, like Miz Mimosa, too. Mama had some magic to her. She had a way that she could bring money right out of the ground."

"Iona, what in the world are you talking about?" Addie, as tired as she was, perked up, astounded.

"Uh-huh, she did. One time she sent me under this ol' house over on Pender Street and told me to wait fo' the money to come up. But, Lord, I come out so fast. I saw ol' hosses' heads and soldiers coming up out of that dirt. She grabbed me and said, 'You get back under there, the money comin' up now,' and there it was. All these old coins." Iona looked placidly at her fingernails.

"Oh, Iona, hush, I don't believe a word of that."

"True though, and she could make hair grow on yo' head, too. Go out in the woods and gets these ol' pieces of barks and stuff, boil it all in a kettle and plum cure a bald head 'bout overnight."

"Iona!"

"Give her recipe away, though. Wish'd I'd a got it.

You know, Miss Addie, everybody got some magic in theirselves. Just shows up in different ways. Yo mama, she had plenty of magic in her, too."

"Yeah, I remember trying to use the Ouija board with her once. That planchet ran all over the board every time she touched it. It was like she was full of electricity. She promised she wasn't moving it, and Langley maintains she broke his car down once when he wanted to drive out to Washington State with some boys to pick asparagus. Broke it right down, he said, because she didn't want him to go so far." Addie's face was smoothing as she spoke, and she smiled across the table at Iona.

"Uh-huh, and I seen her feeding squirrels right out of her hand. They come right up to her, her sitting out there on them back steps. And, Lord, those birds, all around her when she stood out there watering her bushes, all taking baths and carrying on." Iona looked, bright-eyed, into Addie's eyes.

"I heard about the sea gulls, Iona," Addie laughed.

"Uh-huh, that was funny. Least they didn't come home with her."

Iona was quiet for a few minutes, drinking her coffee. "Miss Addie, your mother love you and Mr. Langley. She just couldn't see none of her in you so much. Just like, you didn't see none of her in you."

"Do you think she was ever happy, Iona?"

Iona looked sadly at Addie. "She loved them birds and her yard and the river and both you twins, and, Miss Addie, get right down to it, happiness just liking where you at."

"Her cardinals, things like that, I suppose, and loving the littleness of it all. She was like Daddy in that. I guess she never thought I would fetch up at the same place." Addie's red eyes filled with tears. "Too late to tell her."

"You don't haf to tell her. She know, in the end I bet she do."

*

Winter Goldfinch

**Part VIII
April**

Jayne Davis Wall

Winter Goldfinch

Spring Fever

Addie and Franklin sat on a bench in the little park just down the hill from Mimi's house on the river. Late March had arrived with a mixture of warm sun and rain showers, but the crepe myrtle arbor was bare still. A fretwork of rich brown twining twigs and vines just beginning to glow reddish with the promised buds of honeysuckle leaf. Last year's grass was brown all around where it wasn't covered with dark dry leaves and pine straw, but the sun filtering through the bare oak branches was comfortably warm on their backs, and they both tied their heavy sweaters around their shoulders to bask idly as they watched their dogs sniffing and snuffling nearby.

"They look like pigs trained to root out truffles, don't they? Just a couple of little piggies." Addie laughed.

"Yeah. I wish we could do this more. They get so excited getting away from the same old thing, but Sunday's the only day I really have, and even then . . . " Franklin's voice trailed off. "I wish I could see you more." He smiled and turned up his collar. "This sun is deceptive. My neck's a little coolish."

"Don't be tragic, Franklin. We see each other a lot." Addie laughed at him and began to pull her sweater back over her head. They both smoothed her static-stricken hair until it lay quiet and orderly in place again.

"You know what I mean."

Franklin looked out toward the road winding through the park at a man and woman strolling along holding hands with each other and, with their free hands, the hands of two children, a boy and a little girl. A cocker spaniel ran ahead of them. "Uh oh, hey! Andrew, come here boy. Fitz!" The obedient Andrew came up wagging his tail but it was too late to stop Fitz. "Hold Andrew. I'll get him. Fitz! Come back!"

Franklin ran, but Fitz, running flat out was faster and on top of the oblivious cocker before anybody could react, and, amid the frightened screams of the children and the furious terrier and collie barking, the spaniel, alone, showed the calmness of good sense.

She rolled over, silken ears flopping on the road, her front feet in prayer position, her back feet hanging open and vulnerable. Fitz stopped, sniffed, wagged his tail and trotted back, dragging his lead, to meet Franklin.

"I'm so sorry. He jerked right away from us. I should know better. Damn terriers. Is she all right? I'm a veterinarian, if you want me to check her over?" Franklin stood red-faced, and, as Addie and Andrew approached, she thought he looked extremely handsome and disarming.

His stance seemed to be working for him, she thought, because the man smiled and said, "It's okay. We should have had ours on a leash, too, but she's met these warrior dogs before. She knew what to do. She's fine. Don't worry."

Winter Goldfinch

There seemed to be nothing else to say so Addie and Franklin, dogs firmly in hand, turned to walk away.

"I don't like your dog," the little girl shrilled. "He's mean!"

"I know. I'm sorry," Addie answered contritely.

And, then, the little boy, peeping out from behind his mother stuck out his tongue. "Yeah," he said, "and he stinks, too!"

"Oh, what do you know, you little squirt?" Addie, giggling, whispered to Franklin, and they began walking in the direction of the bench in the sun.

They didn't stop but continued walking along the path that ran by the creek, which now had a fair-sized trickle down its middle from a short heavy rain early that morning.

"Your dog. What a beast." Franklin lifted his elbow and nudged Addie in her arm.

"Love me. Love my dog."

"Hey, you know me. I'm a vet. I get paid to love all dogs, great, like Andrew, and small, like Fitz. With Fitz, though, there's some kind of big bully dog in there trying to get out."

"He just talks big."

Addie was thinking of something else as they walked through the lacy sun and shadow of the early spring afternoon.

Franklin reached out and took her hand, and Addie looked up at him and then dipped her head to his shoulder, resting it there for a moment. "It's just so much has happened since I've been home . . . I . . . ." Addie looked down at her feet. They stopped walking.

"I know. Don't worry. I'll be here . . . ." Franklin flushed pink and said, "Things never just stop, though, you know." He paused. "Cherry's going to have a baby."

"Oh! When?"

"In the fall. Late October or early November, I think. She didn't say exactly." Franklin pushed at the pine straw on the path with the toe of his shoe.

"You must be so happy, Franklin," Addie smiled and tried to keep a cold remoteness that suddenly gripped her from chilling her voice.

She brushed his cheek with her fingers and reached up to give him a quick peck on his lips, but he put his free arm around her neck and buried his face in her hair. "Happy and a little sad and scared."

"Yes," she said and slipped her arm around his waist, and they slowly moved along the path by the creek, feeling their bodies fitting warmly together through the sweaters and the jeans and the sun, cooling some, coming around to hit them now and beginning to shine in their eyes. Their thoughts did not become words again until they said, almost at the same time, "It's getting dark. Let's go home," and they turned back to walk the way they came.

*

Winter Goldfinch

Spring Epilogue

May finally brought one of those springs when everything seemed to come together at once. The grass in Mimosa's back yard was greening again. Buttercups and clover, henbit and meadow mint were everywhere and the violets were beginning under the trees.

A soft breeze was lifting the dark straight hair on Adeline's forehead. She was lying in the old Hatteras hammock under the pear trees. An opened book lay in the grass beside her. She was dreaming. A long slow dream.

She felt herself, strolling in slow motion, deep in a blizzard of bluebirds. This time she was in the middle of the meadow. Blue wings were gently brushing her face and hands as the birds plunged softly into the flowered grass and rose again. She could smell the honeysuckle along the verge of the woods against which the meadow lay nestled. Somewhere a wood thrush fluted its liquid song.

In her dream she knew she was happy at last.

She smiled and looked towards the trees. There John stood waving with one hand and holding her beautiful lost baby cradled in his other arm, the both of them fading back into the wood and, with them, she saw Daddy scattering white flowers like stars and waving too. Last, Lillian and Mimi, holding hands and blowing little kisses at each other and at her.

She smiled again and Franklin appeared wading through the grass, parting the bluebirds, and his hands were full of snowflakes, which he sprinkled on her upturned face as he laughed and laughed, but the snow tickled and Adeline opened her eyes, still smiling.

Snow was everywhere—on her face and clothes, on the grass and on the book. She laughed and blew the snowy petals of the pear tree into the warm air, holding her hands as if she, too, were blowing kisses, yawned, picked up her book and, still smiling, began to read.

Acknowledgements

Many thanks to the River Walk Writers Circle, early readers Marni and Jake, and to all the others who read and listened to me discuss ad-nauseam the earliest stages of this book. Thanks to Joe Davis and Whiting Toler for talking to me about the "holes" and to Anna and Judy who helped so much with the typing and the computer.

And, Sam, Stephan and Bev, without you . . . nothing.

Jayne Davis Wall writes and paints in Eastern North Carolina where she lives with her husband, Sam, and their many dogs and cats.

*

17.